SHERWOOD

SHERWOOD

A Story of an Empathetically Reluctant Hero
(or ...Misunderstood Hero)

JONATHAN RIIKONEN

To order additional copies of this book, contact:
Xlibris
1-888-795-4274
www.Xlibris.com
Orders@Xlibris.com
765077

SHERWOOD

SINCE I HAVE time now, I thought of writing down some of my thoughts, memories, and occurrences when I still remember them almost like yesterday. I don't want to think my life has been extraordinary; it's just one different life, that's all. All lives matter, and every person on the planet has an exciting and unique life.

I am not very good at writing. We all have faults, and maybe I'll turn more fluent along the way, but I hope you can gather my feelings at least from between the lines and understand my basic message, namely, beyond a person's appearance, there is always an unseen microcosm of emotions, opinions, and personal choices. I guess I don't need much to be happy. I just need the right things, but fame and money are not among them.

The thing about life is that it doesn't always go as we dreamed it. I never planned or wanted to be a hero, but I was pushed into heroism. I never wanted to become famous, but stardom chased me. I didn't think I would settle down with a partner, but it just happened.

I never really wanted to become rich, but money offers kept pouring in. It was the least of my problems though. I never enjoyed any sport or any physical activity. To me, it was a futile thing and a waste of time, except for jousting and fencing maybe—good old medieval pursuits. I adored books, languages, Eastern philosophies, ancient history, astronomy, and mythology.

I loved my first adult job as a crane operator. It was a free and fabulous job where you virtually could be your own supervisor. Sometimes I wonder why everybody didn't want to work with cranes, but then again, not everybody wanted to become an oceanographer or gravedigger either. I had dreams, dreams of becoming happy and just being an ordinary, unrecognized citizen, but perhaps I will always be remembered, at least in record books. It all started as suddenly as it ended.

Well, finally, I found my happiness and peace but literally in a very accidental way. Someone who doesn't know me could call it a brutal or unfair way, but I see it differently. It was actually a reassuring soul-searching experience. This is a story, my story. A story with a beginning, a middle, and an end. I'd be relieved to forget the middle, except for when I met Gina, but I guess these things are meant to occur, just like things in your life must happen.

*   *   *

It all starts—our journey, I mean—when we are born. We don't remember it personally, but moms, godparents, and grandparents have told us, and we have photo albums or files, also coloring books and our first drawings. Our moms saved paint a picture of our youth. It was the happiest time of our lives because we didn't need to take care of anything—not to plan schedules, not to worry what to wear, when to wake up, or to count calories. Under Mom's wings and guidance, all went spontaneously and naturally.

I remember, or maybe I only remember a picture my aunt had taken, how I played a catch-it game with my mom. I was maybe two years old or actually two years young. She would shoot little plastic buttons from a gadget with a spring, like a bazooka that sends satellites into their orbit. There were buckets you tried to shoot them into, but instead, she made me catch them. I think it was fun since my mom told me it made me burst with joy every time.

JONATHAN RIIKONEN

I was clumsy at first, she said, but soon I developed an amazing hand-eye coordination and would catch those little flying saucers from midair when they passed by. It almost became my second nature, no matter which hand I used. Maybe this trained me to what I was to become later. Yes, I guess I had some good catches that commentators and sportswriters called amazing, marvelous, flabbergasting, magical, miraculous, inimitable, otherworldly, incomprehensible, or even surreal. If anything, I would call my mother with some of those attributes. I think she made me a star, but then again, I don't really know.

"Okay, Sherwood, Mommy will make you some lunch now," she used to say.

Even though I liked, and still like, all my mother's cooking, there was something I really loved all through my life. It was oatmeal porridge and apricot jam. The way she let it stew slowly on the stove after cooking and her secret condiments made it indescribably delicious.

I could have her oatmeal porridge on Thanksgiving or Christmas Eve as my main course when I was younger, and even now, it is still a perfect lunch for me. In the backyard, we had three apricot trees, and my mom made jam with her old grandma's recipe. I loved it much more than candy or Coke, which other kids devoured. The oatmeal porridge and the apricot jam made a perfect combination, a culinary delight.

My father was not around. Who was he, I never got to know. I never saw a picture because it happened in the dark, I figure. My mom never mentioned him; she only told me about my ethnic origin, and I grew up wondering, not wanting to ask any questions. I felt I was the man of the house from the very beginning. I wished I had a little brother or sister, but luckily, I met Bob in the second grade when he moved to my neighborhood. We grew up together in a brotherly spirit. Our one daring pursuit was to walk along the railway track, balancing on the rails. A few times, a train came so close that they used the siren to drive us off. We would run away laughing.

Otherwise, we were different. Like they say, opposites attract. He was ambitious, wanting to become something big. I was only interested in old history, books of knowledge, languages, astronomy, and such. Bob liked to play anything: soccer, street hockey, basketball, running, and jumping. I never was keen to any of them, and I never dreamed of becoming famous. It's just that we people are individuals with different callings, preferences, and cravings. Well, Bob was also interested in chemistry.

We had a big backyard with long grass that I was supposed to cut twice a month. That was my exercise besides carrying out the garbage and raking the autumn leaves. So our neighborhood boys and one girl used it as a soccer field on Saturdays. I used to study alchemy or languages or stars and constellations. I guess I never was a child in that sense like the others. Well, big boys and girls also play ball games sometimes for big money.

My mother always sent me to the veranda, as she called the back terrace, because she didn't want to see anyone there when she was cleaning the house.

"Look, you are in my way. Go and join your friends!"

When I took my books along and went to the veranda chair, she would semisarcastically remind, "Watch out not to sprain your page-turning finger."

I still knew she supported my hunger for knowledge. The only nuisance was that there were bugs, but luckily, I could use my quick hand movements to catch them, thanks to my mom's catch-it game when I was a toddler.

A couple of times a ball would bounce into the terrace, and if I could reach it, I would kick or throw it back. Many times Bob wanted me to join them, but I declined. I was utilizing my free will. At physical education class in school, we had to do things that I could not avoid, and as a result, I got my only D beside a full flush of As in my report card. If we had had medieval-style fencing, I might have taken it seriously. It needs coordination of a quick hand and a sharp eye.

In my neighborhood, some folks spoke Spanish, French, Polish, Yiddish, or even Greek. I used to listen to them speaking and picked up words here and there. This urged me to study the languages of my ancestry. My background was Sami from Lapland, Finnish, Basque, Welsh, and Sanskrit—yes, my paternal grandfather had been a rare white person speaking Sanskrit, which only about eleven thousand still speak at the foot of Himalayas. Later on, I decided one day I would move there and learn all about cultivating green tea, perhaps in the Darjeeling area.

I don't know why learning languages was so easy to me. Maybe I subconsciously created my own method how to memorize the words, grammar, and sentence structures, and my ear told me what was correct. In about every three months, I could adopt a new language, and by the age of twelve, I already spoke ten languages fluently. I didn't brag with them but did it just for self-satisfaction. If I heard someone speaking one of them, I might say something funny to surprise them.

Most of the languages were simple, but somehow my ancestors had chosen some of the most difficult ones in the world. I liked Latin, the mother tongue of Romans and one base of modern English and Romance languages. It was a clear language since you always knew how to spell a word you have heard, just like many others in the world. Also, spoken Latin was extinct, but it was still very much alive in botany, zoology, medicine, and other sciences.

I had really to immerse in Finnish, Sami, Welsh, and Basque, while Sanskrit was just a logical piece of cake. See, for example,

Finns can say any noun in fifteen different ways, depending on the context, and they can add suffixes to a noun, like personal pronouns and negative endings, making words long. For example, "Even without causing any chaos by himself" would simply translate as *epäjärjestelmällistyttämättömyydelläänkään*. Or if you add *moon* and *earth* or "kuu" and "maa," you get a word that means "hot."

The Basque tongue, Euskara, was similar with even four endings, with also different male and female suffixes in one word. Its speech sounds consist of both apico-alveolar and predorsal sibilants, and then they have corresponding affricates or *tz* sounds, but *balatals xx* also exist. Like the sentence "I give it to her" is only one word in Basque with four personal markers, Bazekarzkionat, which contains a singular subject "t," third person plural direct object "zki," third person singular indirect predicative "o," as well as female addressee of the utterance "na." Perhaps that makes more sense to you now.

And then there was Sami with personal forms for one, two, and many, plus other intriguing grammatical tongue twisters. The Welsh, in turn, has masculine and feminine forms for numbers, like 2 can be *dau* or *dwy*, depending on the context, or 16 literally means "1 on 15" or *un ar bymthag*.

Why do we need to know languages we would possibly never need? Why do some people want to learn origami or belly talking or do rock climbing or keep bees? It can be an inner calling, this unexplainable power that urges our free will to choose. Sometimes it can be an accident or a coincidence in which one thing leads to another and so on. Speaking of which, one epoch-making coincidence and its consequences dominated my life for a good part.

My school years were simply too easy for me. I did my math book in a week and science tasks in two, so Teacher let me read scientific and history books and sometimes made me tutor the others. It was a little

JONATHAN RIIKONEN

frustrating since they hardly ever comprehended my reverse approach and converse logic of how things could be done. I was not a genius. I just used not solely common sense but the brain's full potential to my benefit.

The most peculiar thing to me was how history was taught at school. Okay, we were kids, but still, I needed to make my point. One day we talked about the pyramids, those colossal cone-like ancient Egyptian stone monuments. When our teacher, naively in my opinion, claimed that they were nothing but tombs of pharaohs, I had to interrupt.

Talking about the Great Pyramid or Pyramid of Cheops, I first reminded them that there's no mention of Cheops or Khufu in Egyptian, and they have never found his remains from the building. Some say the pyramid was a grain silo; some others, a space lighthouse, while still others believe it was a giant battery of earth energy, a sanctuary for fertility rites, or only a dead pile of rocks telling the world about the might of their king. I even know how they were built.

When Teacher denied everything categorically, I asked permission to get in front of the class, and she somehow reluctantly gave in. I went to explain that the Great Pyramid was actually a mathematical reminder of ancient high civilization, way higher than Egypt where an abacus was the most advanced calculator.

I started with the facts using metric system.

"For example, if you take two base lengths divided by the height, you will get pi. Its height is ten-billionth part of the average distance between the earth and sun, and the pyramid's location 29.9735 degrees north is exactly the same as the speed of light in kilometers per second and—"

At that point, Teacher rose and approached, exacerbated.

"How do you know that? They must be pure coincidences," she said, red-faced.

I just added, "All 153 of them? So far, I've only explained three of them!"

She retorted, "Sherwood, don't argue with your teacher. It's nothing but a tomb, all the people know that. Now go and sit down!"

"Yeah, they foolishly think they know," I quipped and went back to my seat.

Anyway, we were in the sixth grade now, and I was two years younger than the others. Maybe it was after this or any other similar argument, like once we talked about Romans, and Teacher taught as a sure fact that the Roman Empire collapsed because it became too difficult to control. Actually, it was well organized, and when all the vassals were given different rights or benefits, they actually competed with one another for the favors of the central government in Rome.

The real reason or one main contributor, even though very few want to acknowledge it, is the fact that all the people of intelligence—military leaders, teachers, and high officials—withered from lead poisoning. The upper class lived in the part of Rome with plumbing and running drinking water via lead pipes. This eventually ate up their brains and made them dull and incompetent to educate, lead, or create strategies. This one also the teacher repealed strongly because he did not have any clue.

So after one of those debates, Bob invited me to see his test lab in their basement. He had received a basic chemical experiment kit as a gift from his uncle. This led to expand his collection of elements, test tubes, and knowledge of the subject. Again, a good example how one thing can lead to another and spark a new hobby and, in his case, eventually a career too. But I only learned this much later.

With Bob, we walked through the normal route, Orbit Street, the other main road of Jonesboro, California, an outermost suburb of Santa Barbara. They were constructing a ten-floor building with two cranes in the site. I often had to stop and admire those operators high up there and how expertly they handled those loads. I felt it was a free job and the second closest to working on high air besides being a pilot or astronaut.

Although I was into books and philosophy, I felt a crane operator would be a perfect job. When there were breaks, I could read my books, appreciate the view, and be alone in my own microcosm. My other grandpa was a gravedigger, but I was just the opposite. I desired to be high above the ground. I told Bob my school project would one day be a crane operator's day.

"Right, Sherwood! With all your knowledge, you should be a university teacher, or you could become Socrates and Einstein in one," he stated.

I just said I wanted to be modest and have an independent yet humble job.

On the window of a family store, there was a sign that the California lottery had a $48 million jackpot. Bob became eager.

"If I won this, I'd buy a moon rocket or Rolls-Royce or a well-equipped lab with that or something."

I told him I would not like to win it. Why? Because I think people are much happier with less. In the old days, most people had little money, but they were contented.

Bob thought I was crazy and explained, "Because they didn't know any better. My goal is to become famous and rich, maybe a Nobel laureate chemist."

I wished him good luck. I don't know how something told me that I would have more money than I ever needed, but as for now, I shrugged it off. But why must so many people dream of accumulating lots of money when life is full of much more important things?

At Bob's place, he told me not to take off my shoes since his lab floor had multicolored spots here and there, and the whole quarters had a funny, pungent smell. He poured us sodas into earless china cups he picked from the drying rack. Then he opened a little cabinet, took a big test tube and holder, and put the contraption on the desk. Then we rummaged through the ingredients, actually elements.

"Saturated neon water," I exclaimed. "One of alchemists' favorites!"

We added stuff into the tube randomly, and almost every time, the color changed, and it emanated different smells. We put everything from tungsten dioxide and iodine carbonate to aspirin and castor oil. Once, it started to froth a little, but when we added some unknown tincture, it abated. I knew from medieval alchemy how they could make secret potions to get strength in battles, live longer, or even create gold, as they claimed.

We had lots of exciting fun together. We felt like bakers or lemonade industrialists, inventing a new dough or drink. After a while, we decided it was ready. The sweet-smelling concoction had a light greenish-greyish-pinkish color, just like my pink grapefruit–Dr Pepper soda mix. Next, Bob poured it into a cup, similar to the ones he had on his rack.

Then I helped him clean up the desk and floor. We sat down, and he opened a packet of cookies, luckily my favorite, oatmeal. We took our sodas, and as soon as I had a big gulp, something strange happened. All of a sudden, I went dizzy, but at the same time, I felt a titillating heat wave going through my body. I saw twinkling stars on the walls and ceiling, and my heart pounded for a while like a marathoner's.

"I think now we should . . . should go to see if the turquoise cow auctioneer has negotiated a better price for the mint helicopter."

That's exactly what I said according to Bob. Then he had grabbed my sleeve and pulled me outside. After breathing long and deep the fresh spring air, I felt normal.

"Must have been the smell of the poison we made," my classmate said, and he went down to clean the cups.

I still don't know what exactly happened to me. Was the soda somehow flattened or had turned bad? I don't want to think it was those vapors we might have inhaled.

On my way home, I saw a young mother pushing her baby's pram stop when her phone rang. Somehow my instincts told me to glance above, and I noticed a flowerpot was falling from a balcony straight above the baby. I reacted lightning fast and caught it in the nick of time. I set it on the canopy of the carriage and continued. Bob witnessed my act with mouth agape. The mother never saw it, but maybe she wondered later who had donated her a flower. It was not a big deal, and I'm not sure if I even mentioned it to my mom.

*　　*　　*

This season, I decided to do also the seventh, eighth, and ninth grade final tests even though our principal claimed it was impossible. But I studied in my free time, and came June, I had straight As in every topic. Now the proud principal talked about a child prodigy even though it all was logic and the questions were so easy that even a child could have answered them. I decided that during the summer holiday, I would study the next three grades.

To my chagrin, Bob's family had to move to Maine, the other side of the continent. His father was in the navy's marine guard unit, and when he got the order, they had to pack their stuff, load them into a navy aircraft carrier, and move to the northeast. I helped Bob pack his chemical stuff, his sporting equipment, and his favorite clothes. His mom took care of the rest. Our farewell was quite quick: no hugging, no exchanging of addresses or numbers, just a "See ya!" and that was it.

Next season, I turned thirteen on February 13. My mom always said she wanted to wait for one more day to have a Valentine's Day child, but I was eager to come out. By then, I had done my equivalent of English matriculation examination, more than a US high school diploma. Now I could concentrate on my hobbies, like reading more. I realized I hadn't even read *The Great Gatsby, Moby Dick, For Whom the Bells Toll, Grapes of Wrath, Uncle Tom's Cabin*, or *Tropic of Capricorn* yet. I corrected this deficiency rapidly.

My history answers, the teacher confessed later, had taken him a fortnight to verify, but I was right about the origins of Native Americans, the secrets of Incas, Sanskrit's influence to Old English, the Druids, Etruscans, Mesopotamians, Plato's Atlantis theory, and many others. I didn't have time to argue with teachers during the lessons anymore since I wanted to get ahead, and besides, it was fruitless anyway. But I made the teachers work hard to verify the facts I sometimes laid on the table.

The rest of the season, I concentrated on new languages. I studied Arabic, Khmer, Japanese, Turkish, and Farsi, a modern Persian. Because of their own writing, it took me more time than I expected, but by the end of summer, I was good in twenty-three languages. Next, I decided to concentrate on some Native American tongues and also learn more about astrophysics and natural nutrition.

I enrolled in the Jonesboro Enviro College where all my peers were at least nineteen years old. I was, by far, the shortest of all guys and also tinier than a few girls, and I was soon called Dwarfie. Out of the twelve subjects, only one, environmental engineering, was in the curriculum; besides, we had to choose five other subjects we liked. Well, I could not decide, so I took them all, except physical education because I claimed that I was too small and that my lungs were not good. They were, in fact, excellent; but because of they didn't have fencing or yoga, I decided physical activity was not for me.

Our French teacher was sickly, and often I was called to substitute him. I liked it, especially since they paid me $28 per hour. Soon I offered to substitute all the teachers. For the other students, I was a peculiar character, I guess. I felt first they overlooked me, but at the same time, appreciated the extra knowledge I brought to them. At nights, I would study the twenty-four-piece encyclopedia through, but I realized there was so much to add, change, and omit. But it was just fun to play with the thought. After the second season, I had passed all the final tests and also learned five more languages: Swahili, Aramaean, Sioux, Mongolian, and Apache. I left the Enviro College two years ahead of the rest. Now I was fifteen and much taller than when I started.

*   *   *

The turning point in my own career was again watching the cranes operating in a nearby lot. Jonesboro was growing quickly, and a construction boom kept the town busy. In the second year, I decided I would apply as a trainee in the summer and then perhaps become a full-time operator. One day in May, I went to the office of the area's biggest builder, Pro-Construction or Pro-Con. I liked the dual meaning of its short name since *pro* means "for something" and *con* "against something."

I had imagined there was a long list of candidates, but actually, there wasn't. I was told that many applicants have rushed down trembling, pale faced, or with a loose stomach after experiencing the cabin 120 feet up, swaying in the wind and bending under heavy weights like a house of cards. I was out of breath because of climbing but loved the very first moment up there. I admired the view, loved the swinging, and saw how routinely but accurately the pilot, Mr. Hartvale, handled the loads.

Because of my age, unfortunately, I was only allowed to train up there, not to operate alone. Many loads we lifted and lowered down, from every floor and angles possible. Before I even realized, it was lunch hour. I wanted to spend it up in the air, but nature called, and I had to climb down. I was now at the brink of my dream occupation.

When I opened my box of oatmeal porridge and apricot jam, the other guys in the lunchroom laughed, not viciously, but heartily. Mr. Hartvale had ten sausage sandwiches and a big container of coffee. He had been operating it eight years and could not anymore imagine any other job. In the afternoon, it was my turn to try moving loads, and I was as excited as a young colt on his first day in the meadow. I knew this was my calling, a dream job come true. That day, I felt I was fully learned, but then came the hard part. After finishing, we had to service the engine, oil the moving parts, and clean the pulleys. I took it as a necessary evil.

After training, I was offered a ground job, running errands, shoveling earth, and taking care of garbage cans. By lunch hour, I was exhausted and told my boss that I sprained my back. They sent me home but told me to report back when I turned sixteen. I don't even know how I did those eight months. I think I spent lots of time in the library and at the computer, scouring for information about anything. Also, I was called at least a dozen times to substitute for some teachers, once a full week for our physics professor.

Finally, February 13 came, and I was allowed to have a driver's license and, thus, also operate a crane. The same morning, I signed up at work where they were already expecting me. I was offered another shorter crane in Pro-Con's other work site. They were expanding the six-story hospital and had just had erected this brand-new eighty-eight-feet-high load lifter, the Boom Boy. It was to become my second home for a while. I named it Aerie as I felt it was like an eagle's nest up there.

From experience, I knew there would be some extra time, so I brought a book written in old church Latin and also a magazine of super sudokus to kill time. Besides them, I brought a little player and my baroque music collection. Sometimes I was busy two hours in a row, and sometimes I had fifteen-minute breaks after one or two loads. Construction is never plain sailing.

I also decided to buy a pair of binoculars or maybe a telescope with my first salary. That day, I went home with eyes sparkling and told my mom all about my job. I was now a real man of the house, another breadwinner and trusted employee of a big company. I already knew I would retire from my job some fifty years later. My future was set— well, that's what I believed.

The next four or five years went like that. I got to know the other guys who had basically four topics for their lunch breaks: sports, politics, women, and then some more sports. I never knew what they were talking about since I read books.

"Hey, Sherwood, what do you think? Who will win the Super Bowl this season?" asked one guy.

"What is it? Bowling or horse-trotting trophy or what?" I asked at a loss, lifting my eyes from the book.

They laughed at me, and another guy hinted that the only sport I knew was knitting. I just didn't care.

There were a few athletic-looking guys in Pro-Con payroll, and they had formed a recreational hockey league team. The guys played against other companies and hobby club teams on the weekends and occasional late nights. Since Jonesboro had only one ice arena, it was hard to get training time. Pro-Con's only slot was at five on Wednesday morning. I was happy I didn't have to participate. In the recreational hockey series, Pro-Con had lost all but their one game. It was mostly because of their not-so-good goalie, I had heard, but they didn't have a choice, and it was only rec hockey anyway.

* * *

Then one day it happened. It was Thursday late afternoon, and they were supposed have a game at eight. The guys were leaving when Billy, their team captain, rushed in.

"Hey, guys, we are in trouble. Wayne just had a burst appendix, and he was taken to hospital. We need a replacement goalie quick. Sherwood!"

He looked at me like his life depended on this.

I couldn't believe my own ears: me?

"Are you crazy? With bare hands? I don't even know any ice hockey rules!" I protested.

"Don't worry, we will give you pads. And there is only one rule: you stop all the pucks that are shot against you. Thanks for doing this. You are the best."

This said, he went and left me in wonderment. Another player, Don, promised to pick me up at seven. I regretted my promise, but after all, I wanted to do it for my company, which gave me the greatest job on earth.

So I asked my mom to make me oatmeal porridge, and I ate two platefuls with apricot jam with a big glass of soy milk. I needed it for encouragement. I could sense my mom was worried but proud of me the same time. I was really scared, uncertain, and apprehensive; it was not my alley at all. Don came exactly at seven, and I jumped into his pickup truck. On our way, he explained me some game strategies and what I was supposed to do. The last game they had lost, 2–7, and they already expected another loss, I could sense it from his sentimentality.

At the dressing room, I didn't have a clue how to wear those goalie pads. Billy helped me put them on, and fifteen minutes before the H-hour, we all skated onto the ice to have a little warm-up first. I had roller-skated a couple of times when I was young, so I could keep my balance, but I was relieved when I could lean against the goal frame.

JONATHAN RIIKONEN

They guys skated around to warm up and shot some easy ones against me. I felt it was similar to catching the flies before with my bare hand when I picked a puck after another.

Then the game commenced. The series-leading Dragonslayers started to attack, and soon there was a fusillade of shots. It was very easy to pick them up or veer them away with my stick. For half an hour, they tried their best shots, but it was no problem for me. In the end, our team scored two lucky ones, and we won, 2–0. After the end whistle, all the guys came to congratulate me and told me how amazing I had been. I was embarrassed and felt I had only done my one-time assignment as requested.

Our next game was on Sunday morning at eight. Since Wayne was still recovering, they dragged me to that one too. I insisted that there must be another guy, but it was out of the question. They told me I was the best and their only hope. So even though I disliked any sports activity, I had to yield again.

Now I knew how to put my protective gear on by myself, and my skating to the goal was easier. This time the opponent didn't have very good goalie either, I guess, since he allowed a quick goal in the first minute. Then the opponent, Wendy's Burgerboys, started to press, and by halftime, I had stopped twenty-seven shots already. In the second half, our guys had two more, and for my part, I did what they made me do: kept my goal clean.

Again, they all surrounded me, tapping my back and praising my performance. To me, it was just nothing more significant than a catch-it game I played with my mom. Somehow, to my surprise, I wasn't tired at all after the games; my muscles felt as relaxed as after a regular workday. All I needed was a cup of water. At home, my mom was so happy even though I said it was only a vain little boy's silly game.

I wanted to quit after every game, but they would not allow me. Even the company president came and shook hands with me after I had had my fifth shutout. Pro-Con was climbing in the standings; we were third now. I never went to early morning or any other practices because it was easy just to stand there and pick or fend off pucks. We still had eight games to play, and they even let us leave an hour earlier during the game nights. The guys talked about hockey at lunch breaks, but it was boring and a distraction to me. I was studying now my thirty-eighth language, a native Guatemalan's indigenous tongue.

Two games later, we had a rare game at three o'clock on Saturday afternoon. The company had arranged a picnic, and all ninety employees came with families to cheer for us. It was a weird feeling to be the center of attention. Someone held a sign "Go, Sherwood! Go, Pro-Con!" and my mom was so proud of this even though I had reminded her that to me it was all vanity. The game went routinely. My team scored three goals, and I stopped some forty-seven shots and kept my record 100 percent. After it was over, they cheered, like seeing Elvis onstage. I hated it and was embarrassed to be in the spotlight.

Yes, eventually, we won the championship because we had beaten all the teams still ahead of us. I made saves, like snatching the bugs from the veranda. It was Pro-Con's first title, and even our suburb paper, *Jonesboro Harbinger*, covered the last game. Our company had a big party, and I was the guest of honor although I insisted I never scored; it was my teammates who did all the physical work.

But they let me choose a menu, so we had a company dinner of oatmeal porridge and apricot jam. You should have seen their faces after expecting, I guess, beef, asparagus, mashed potatoes, and pumpkin pie with whipped cream. I was only glad that the series was over, and I could resume my daily routines and be a private person again.

JONATHAN RIIKONEN

I need to add, there was something that I had noticed in our last two games. Since I had time to look around when the puck was on the other side of the rink, I had paid attention to one pin-striped fellow sitting in the stands at the goal line with notebook in hand, and he also seemed to take a few pictures. I thought he was a local enthusiast or newspaperman or something. Well, soon I realized he was somebody else, a "big shot," someone would say.

But by winning a championship with such a great margin, our team was invited to the national rec league champions' tournament in Kansas City. I was not planning to go, but then the Pro-Con company president talked me over it. He stressed it was actually an unwritten part of my work contract and responsibility toward the company. Again, in his eyes, I was the best and our biggest hope and blah-blah, so somehow reluctantly, I yielded but gave a condition: I needed my own hotel room to be able to read and sleep when I wanted. Surprisingly, that was granted.

On the plane to Kansas City, I realized how small everything looked from the plane compared from my crane cabin. Must be even more awesome for the astronauts. This made me miss my job badly. When the others learned about my private room, someone quipped about it, but on the other hand, they knew they needed me more than I needed them. I don't say this proudly or selfishly but as a necessary evil fact.

We had two games a day so that all the eight teams could meet once during the first four days. We won them all: 1–0, 3–0, 1–0, 1–0, 2–0, 4–0, 1–0, 1–0. Three times, we had to play overtime to decide a winner. The only difference was, I realized, that the shots came a little harder, and sometimes they had very clandestine two-men breakaways, but I didn't let it distract me. I could tell in advance where they were going to shoot. Besides, I have always wanted to do a good job, so I did now too. I also noticed the same fellow again in the stands following our every game.

There was also local TV station filming and making a story of the tournament and us. After our last game and championships, they came to interview players. I had to answer many nonsense questions.

"Mr. Sherwood, what is your secret? You had eight shutouts in a row, and nobody could even get close to scoring."

All I could tell was that they asked me to keep the pucks out of the goal and I had.

"What kind of a youth hockey career have you had? What is your junior team?"

I told them I didn't have any. I was just a reader, a history buff, and language enthusiast; that's all. They stared at me like they were seeing a unicorn.

*　　*　　*

At night, I retired to my room. I bought some evening snacks, took a shower, and opened a book about ancient astrology. It's amazing how, for example, the Dogon tribe in the African desert of Mali had known two thousand years ago that Sirius was a triple star without telescopes. This was verified only in the 1800s. After just getting cozy, someone knocked on my door. I rose slowly, and before I reached the door, someone knocked even longer and harder. I opened and saw a familiar face, the fellow from the stands. I could sense right away that it meant trouble.

"Hello, I am C. Willie Steele, a lawyer and sports agent."

I nonchalantly asked what he wanted. To me, his name sounded like "See Will He Steal." He said he wanted to become my agent and guaranteed I would land in the NHL, the National Hockey League that is, and make millions. He was, at the same time, overly excited and cold and businessman-like, pretending to be a big benefactor to me.

I answered I was not interested. I was dragged here and that my plays were over, done forever.

"We don't need sports heroism. We need elucidation, deeper harmony, and understanding in this world—and, of course, crane operators."

Then I reminded him it was only a little boy's hobby and of what the old Druids used to say about playing: "You only play trombone at funerals."

He was flabbergasted, I could tell.

"Heck with Druids! Listen to me, you idi—eh, idyllic man. If you don't want glory, your country would. If you don't want money, give it to charity, to your elucidation, or to whatever. The worst you can do is to waste your amazing God-given talent. It's the biggest sin!" he roared.

Those words have been etched in and still haunt my mind. All his pomp had shifted into desperation. Whatever I tried to say, he always argued that this was a tough world and I had to wake up and that he would make me a big star no matter what it needed.

Finally, tired and craving to get back to my book, I yielded and said, "Okay, if it makes you happy!"

He said something sarcastic and instantly picked up a pack of papers and demanded me to sign the last page. Without reading a word, I gave my autograph, and it was not the last autograph in my life. He grinned widely and said that from now on, I was his client and only could talk to him with regard to these matters. I thought, *Whatever*, and went back to my book, relieved I could get rid of him. From the still-ajar door, I saw another man with a briefcase coming, but Mr. Steele stopped him, said a few strong words, showed a document, and he turned around.

The next three weeks went uneventfully. I was happy in my crane cabin where now I solved the most difficult crosswords ever existed. One was so bad that it took me the whole afternoon to solve in between the hoisting tasks. Just when I got to the ground, finishing the workday, my phone rang. It was the same agent, Willie Steele. I had to think for a while before I remembered who he was. I knew that this meant nothing but trouble.

Steele told me to be at the ice arena at eight that night, and I reluctantly went. He was there already with another older gentleman and two NHL hockey players from teams that did not make playoffs. I was introduced to Mr. Nunn, vice president and director of hockey operations for the new expansion team Santa Barbara Igloomakers, and to forward, Terry Liebkind, and defenseman, Kyle Johnson. They wanted to check me out so to speak.

So I put on my hockey armor. Mr. Nunn set his video camera ready, and then by turns, the players started bombarding me from far and close, from all the angles, with slap shots, wrist shots, and backhands. For half an hour, they tried to beat me but did not manage even once. A couple of times I had to stop two pucks the same time, like killing two birds with one stone. Exhausted, these guys begged to get a break, and Nunn decided to wrap it up. I wasn't even sweaty.

"Mr. Steele, I believe we have the biggest golden nugget the hockey world has ever seen. Thank you for your excellent work. If he continues like this, we will make him our number 1 goaltender. You can be sure of that," I overheard.

Wait a minute! I didn't promise to play anymore. I tried to protest and explain it, but it went to deaf ears. Steele gave me a copy of the contract I had signed in which I promised to play in NHL for any team which chooses me. My heart sank, and I was speechless. Why had I signed the paper in the heat of the moment, why?! Now I was chained to my hockey contract who knows for how long. But who knew where I would land? I definitely hoped it would not be far from home like Saskatchewan, Delaware, or Louisiana. Nunn gave me the team trainer's practice instructions, which I ignored. I had never trained before, so why to start now?

The next big date I was really expecting was the weekend of June 27–28. They had a world Sanskrit literary seminar in Concord, New Hampshire, and the president, Kasthrapati Ink, was making a major speech about the prospects of the rare language. I would not miss it for anything. I already had a booked ticket and asked the previous Friday off. Only two days later, Steele called me and reminded me about the NHL draft event in Helena, Montana, on the same weekend. I laconically told him that I was not available at that date.

"Are you crazy? This is the most coveted hockey event, and all the young prospects are proud to be there. You will be picked in the first round for sure!" he bellowed.

I told him I couldn't care less because I already had a reservation. Finally, after an exchange of some words with exclamation marks, he gave up. He promised to arrange Mr. Ink to come and give me a private speech in Jonesboro after the draft weekend. Sadly, I had to settle for that even though I would have loved the atmosphere in that New England conference. Also, now I could not meet any other Sanskrit enthusiasts. Life sometimes treats us unfairly.

Before my Helena trip, I felt stranger than ever. I didn't like any vanity events, and to me, this was a personification of one. The flight went fast because I sat next to an eighty-eight-year-old lady who had lived all her life in modesty until now when her unmarried sister had passed away and left her little money. She was on her way to arrange some things, and this was her second ever flight. She was my hero since she had always lived in modesty. We both agreed too much money was the cause of many problems. I decided to invite her to the company box in one of my games and took her phone number. She only had a landline, not a cell phone.

In Montana for two days, they had a sold-out arena, and they did nothing but select players from different juvenile teams and lower level hockey leagues. Why all the spectators were there beats me. One could waste your valuable free time by doing something more useful. Santa Barbara Igloomakers, as a new expansion team, had the second choice. There were much talked-about duo, Amos Kathmandu and Ulysses Po. Nepal-born defenseman Kathmandu from Quebec Junior League had a six-foot-nine frame and the league's deadliest slap shot. Po, for his part, was only a five-foot-four forward who had ninety-one goals in forty-two games.

Can you imagine people were betting money on who Lexington Ice Derby would choose as number 1! So the Kentucky team Ice Derby chose Po, and when Mr. Stuyvesant, Igloomakers' president, climbed into the podium, all the people expected him to select Kathmandu. The amazement was total when they announced their first ever pick would be Sherwood, me. They didn't even know if it was my first or last name—and it was actually both—but I decided I would never divulge it.

I walked on the stage like a somnambulist, knowing I didn't belong there. I could hear amazed oohs! and whats? from the grandstands. They even had a jersey printed for me with my name, Sherwood, on the back. On the front, it had a hockey player building an igloo with his stick. Our main color would be pink, the first one in NHL's history. This was definitely one of the most embarrassing moments in my life.

In the hotel, I saw the TV reruns where astounded commentators considered Igloomakers' staff total rookies in selecting me. "Sherwood Who?" was a headline even in respected Hockey News. I was just amused about their futile hullabaloo. In the next rounds though, the paper acknowledged they had drafted "some real players." But common prediction was Igloomakers would finish dead last in the league. I didn't care about those hockey experts who were judging before the season even had started.

* * *

I was now officially an NHL player. I went to apologize to my boss that it wasn't my fault that I was leaving the company this coming September, but he totally understood. I even waved off my summer holiday to enjoy every minute of my last two months in the crane cabin. I had more fun than ever. I was happy and didn't want to think too much ahead. I just wanted to enjoy every moment. Toward the end of August, I began to feel melancholic. I didn't know if I could do this job for a long time.

I had to quit when they came to get me to the rookie camp. I hadn't trained the whole summer, except for catching some bugs at home and in my crane cabin. They put the others to lift weights and do pull-ups, but I was exonerated. I told them that I would do it every time when someone scored against me. It wasn't arrogance, but I felt comfortable and knew what I was doing. During the first two days in the seven-day camp, nobody ever scored against me, and after this, I was free to read my books and watch occasional National Geographic Channel programs instead.

There were also young adult girls hanging out, and some of the guys went with them. I had had my time with my neighbor's cousin one summer before, but now I wanted to have my own peace. The league would start three weeks later, and then it was harder to get much privacy. Luckily, I was exonerated from the rest of the practices because

I convinced them I was ready and those young backup goalies needed all the practice time.

I also had to sign a contract that Mr. Steele had negotiated. I don't even know what it read; it was longer than three Declarations of Independence with all kinds of clauses. I only knew I was paid up front $1.5 million, and the rest was based on my performance. I thought that it was outrageous money and bought my mom a new car of her choice and gave $100,000 to the orphanage. Next, I trained with the team half an hour one day before the season opener, and they were happy with me.

That morning, the *Santa Barbara News and Gossip* headlined our Igloomakers' game, "The First Goal to Avoid Last Place in Standings." They referred to me as a National Man of Mystery and wondered if I could withstand all the pressure. I wasn't nervous. I wasn't afraid. I couldn't be more relaxed because I didn't take hockey seriously. The tickets had been sold out weeks before. Soon they named the arena Igloo and referred to us as South Cal Eskimos.

Our first opponent was Cheyenne Beehives, last season's western conference finalist team, that were considered one of the biggest Stanley Cup contenders also for this season. After long opening ceremonies, the game finally started, and soon I faced some hard shots that I could easily kick away or stop with my pads or stick or glove. With every save, the audience cheered. The first twenty-minute period passed, and it was still zero for both. I had stopped nineteen shots, and the opponent's goalie, seven. After the break, our guy, Nick Nantucket, scored the first ever Igloomakers' goal, and the audience went wild.

Toward the end of second period, the Beehives went more and more desperate or should I say, piercing from Bees, and began to shoot even harder, but whatever they did, I just picked the pucks. Our guy scored another goal in the third, and we had won, 2–0. All the players gathered around me like I was a Babylonian demigod. The atmosphere in the

JONATHAN RIIKONEN

audience was festive, but I just wanted to get out of there. But I had to come back because I was chosen the first star of the game. It was just another embarrassing moment to me.

Next, they interviewed me on local and national stations. What could I say, but that I only did my job and it was the teammates who scored. After having stopped fifty-three opponents' shots, the commentators confessed that they had been wrong by criticizing me in the draft and before the game. I said it was okay, I would not blame them. Actually, one sports journalist asked if it was beginner's luck. I said the following games would decide that. They also asked how was I going to celebrate, and I replied I'd have a plate of oatmeal porridge.

Our next game was in Albuquerque against Cactus Huggers. Now I felt my team played with more confidence. They had a new addition, Simon Sandersohn, a six-foot-six center, sturdy like a rock totem, as someone described him. I was warned about his low-area slap shots, but to me, they were easy. I could tell in advance where he was shooting. We only had one goal in the end of the first period.

Then, when Huggers had two minutes left, we had a penalty, and they pulled an extra attacker and left their net empty. The first shot came from close, and I could pick it up like a fly from the left shoulder corner. I took it quickly and hit the puck with a stick like it was a baseball bat. It went straight to the goal. My team went wild. Why? It was just an empty netter goal! So we won again, 2–0, and I had the first star, and the press again asked similar questions and about a rare goalie goal. I said it was just a lucky shot, like David killing Goliath.

That night, we didn't have a curfew until midnight with three beers allowed. Some guys headed to the bar, but I went for a walk to the desert. I usually only sat and read, but now I needed some wind-down time. It was only four blocks from our hotel, at the end of the street. Or maybe it was a park, but there was just sand and cactuses and a couple of dry thorny bushes. The night was clear, and I was wondering and pondering the constellations.

There was Orion with its belt stars: Alnitak, Alnilam, and Mintaka, just like the three pyramids. And there was Pleiades, which the Greek Parthenon was aligned accordingly. The star Lyra seemed almost scintillating. I got back my inner peace little by little. To me, the only real stars were high in the space, not in the sports arenas. I sat there perhaps forty-five minutes and walked back, had some unsweetened soy milk and oatmeal cookies, and went to bed.

From Albuquerque, we flew to Providence. They had an afternoon practice for the next day's game. I was given time off since I hadn't let any goals yet. Rhode Island Manatees had had a disappointing previous season, but now a new coach had brought a new style, and they had scored nine goals in two games already. They predicted a hard night for us, but none of the shot attempts were really threatening.

Once I was lying down when a quick wrist shot came, the guy already raised his hands and the audience cheered, but I just lifted my leg and stopped it with my skate blade in the nick of time. The audience sighed. Now our guys scored three or one in every period. Team captain Adam Chlumskuy had two goals and was selected the first star. I was the second after stopping only twenty-eight shots, the lowest so far. I heard that I had an NHL record for three consecutive shutouts for a rookie and as a season opener the same time. It was not a big deal, I just did my job. I still didn't love it, but I realized now I was okay with it. What was happening? Was I becoming soft already?

Back at home, wherever I went, people kept cheering at me. It was a little nuisance, but I just nodded and continued. To some people, I told I was only a lookalike, and after this, I decided to buy a wig or all-covering cap or something. I walked past a construction site

JONATHAN RIIKONEN

and, without even thinking, walked automatically in. People were so surprised but happy to see me.

There was Wally from our team, and he came to pat me in the back; it was kind of nice to see him. I was happy he wasn't jealous, but I sensed he felt like he had been my mentor. He asked about the big game atmosphere, and I replied I'd rather be operating the crane. He claimed I was incurable. I had four courtesy tickets to the sold-out arena, and I gave them to him and the other guys. Our next game was at home rink on Saturday, two days from now.

I also climbed up the crane and chatted with the operator, a mid-twentyish woman named Lulu. She thought I looked familiar, and when it dawned on her who I was, she was dumbfounded. She let me handle a couple of loads, and I was as excited as in my first day at work. To me, this was the best way to relax and forget all the nonsense hullabaloo around. Lulu told me this used to be her dream job also, but after a while, she wasn't sure anymore. I think I spent two hours there, but it felt like fifteen minutes compared to my toiling on the ice at the goal.

From there, I went to see a couple of apartments with a realtor and found a two-story one not far from city center. It had lots of older-style furniture. I decided to buy it since I had savings and hockey contract money now. I paid the asking price with a check; it was 250 something. I wanted to surprise my mom. The study room in the back would be my library, reading nook, and crossword-filling hideaway.

*　*　*

Now I have been writing my life story a few days, drinking lots of green tea, and eating oatmeal cookies and apricots. I don't know how I am doing so far. I guess my style is a little clumsy since I feel awkward because I think much more fluently compared to writing things down. But this has been a nice experience and challenge. Perhaps toward the end, I'll become more fluent and my text more flowing—unless I get writer's block or something. Don't even know where this text will end up—in the trunk in the attic or become printed—only the time will show. Now I will take a walk in the place I really feel like second home.

Where was I? Oh yes, on Saturday, we had a matinee game that started at 3:00 p.m. We were told that NHL commissioner Gary Putnam would also be there. All of a sudden, lots of outside media and important people were thronging to our games. Well, after all, we were an expansion team and unbeaten so far. I had told the coach, Bartholomew Huggenmuellerstrom, that they can attack more freely and leave goal defending for me, that way I could see the pucks better. Not that it was a problem since I sensed it anyway.

Our game against Fargo Snow Plowers went as usual. The audience cheered every save I made and every shot our guys did. It felt like one big party, except that I didn't feel I belonged there. Lee Bradbury and Brad Lee scored for us in the first period. Then we had to wait until the end of third when we had two more quick ones. Once, Igloomakers, or Eskimos, had two penalties at the same time, and they managed to create six shots during their one-minute, forty-five-second five-on-three effort. Only one shot was bad, since it was a close-range slap shot just above my stick blade into the so-called five-hole or in between the legs, but I stopped it by blocking it with my left pad. The guy was so disappointed, he smashed his stick onto the ice and broke it.

Consequently, we won, 4–0, and an announcer announced that my shutout was again a new NHL record, unseen in its 101-year history. I just shrugged my shoulders; so what, who keeps counting! We still had seventy-eight games left, and I wondered if they were going to celebrate like this every time. At the press conference I gave only one- or two-syllable answers because I felt they knew everything by now. I guess they never thought that stopping the pucks was my second nature.

Santa Barbara News and Gossip already mentioned about Stanley Cup even though the season was just only starting. I heard that Stanley Cup was the most coveted prize and every player's dream. I didn't even know what it looked like, but it didn't interest or bother me a bit. Our next two home games and four-game tour went exactly the same way. We beat Thunder Bay Fish Trawlers from Western Ontario, Canada, 2–0, and Little Rock Roosters, 4–0. Valentino Matuschanaskavasky, who was the only player with a two-line name on his shirt, had a hat trick and the first star to my relief, so they let me mostly alone after the game.

Our road game was tough since in Montgomery, we went overtime at 0–0 and then to shootout before we beat the Moonwatchers. They are the easiest for a goalie since there are no defensemen blocking the view. We won 1–0 after five rounds with Al Moonglow's goal. We also beat Memphis and then Hamilton Odds in East Ontario and Quebec City Francophones in Canada. The Memphis team has a funny name: Elvis Lives.

"Ten Game Shutout Miracle" headlined our home paper the next day. I didn't even read the sports pages, but it has a very challenging half-page super sudoku that took me almost two hours to finish. I learned that in the previous day's paper, they had interviewed my mom. They had asked all kinds of questions like why I was so good and how I was raised. She just said that I was very conscientious whatever I did and, even as a student, wanted always to have a perfect score. Well, except in physical exercise.

I didn't like this kind of a breach of privacy, but when I went over for lamb chops and oatmeal porridge, my mom seemed to be very proud of it, so I let it be. We never confabulate about games; the only thing she wanted to know was if I was all right. I was glad she was so subtle toward me. After the tenth shutout, my agent Steele called me and told that there was a clause in my contract, that reaching the amount, I was to receive half a million bonus and another one after every five more. I just shrugged it off because I never read a line of my contract. I felt that was greediness, but he claimed it was only fair business,

With this, I told my mom that she didn't need to go and work anymore. I paid the last fifty-five thousand of the mortgage off and deposited three hundred thousand to her account. She worked in hospital reception more than part-time, so I would say three-fourths of the time. She was in tears and hugged me. I am not good at hugging, but this felt nice. Now, for the first time, I was contented I was in this position, even though my crane salary had been decent too. The next few days, my mom bought necessary things to my apartment, like a new dresser, some pictures of art, a new shoe shelf for the hallway, and lots of kitchen utensils. I didn't even know I would need a colander or rolling pin.

The Eskimos' next home game was on Monday. The local KRAZ morning news talked widely about the traffic jam it would cause. They gave instructions to those who were coming to the game and to those who didn't have a ticket how to avoid congestion. Our home arena, the Igloo, was in the northeastern side of the city, in the midst of an industrial and office complex area. They also had a guessing contest of how many games I needed until I let the first goal in. The winner was to get a new Jeep. I didn't like big cars myself. Small ones were easier to conduct and park, and besides, to me, a car was just a means of getting from place A to B, not to show off.

As often, they had a light noontime skate, a nap time, and then dinner together three hours before the game warm-up time. At dinner, most guys devoured big steaks and pasta, but I had my oatmeal porridge and a banana split for dessert. My teammates never stopped wondering about my diet. I once told them that, to me, food was not only alimentation but also a great culinary experience. Somehow everyone smiled at me.

After the meal, Coach Huggenmuellerstrom or Huggies as we referred to him behind his back, a well-known baby diaper brand, went through the opponents' strengths and weaknesses. Sometimes the assistant coach, Sid Ek, showed excerpts from the opponents' previous games or from our games, showing the mistakes or fool moves the guys had done. Then we just relaxed and chatted about everyday things. I didn't pay attention to that hockey stuff and let my mind wander but joined them when we left hockey topic behind. I had a Welch language book I kept reading.

I explained to the guys at my table about the curiosities of the Dragon and Big Dipper constellations and also how the Age of Aquarius was connected to its crossing of the Milky Way galaxy. I had no clue why the others didn't get it or even weren't seemingly interested. They only rolled their eyes. I guess playing hockey is simpler than understanding the galactic relations.

Then a bus took us and everyone's big equipment bags to the Igloo. There were about fifty people gathered at the back door to get a glimpse of us; they took photos, and some lucky ones got an occasional autograph. I always wrote my name into twenty pieces of paper and just passed them on for autograph seekers. The trick was I wrote it with a different style every time, so later, they would have a hard time authenticating them; just a silly thought.

In our dressing room, there were new sticks, clean jerseys, and sharpened skates waiting for us. Our staff always did a great job even though they were never really given any compliments for this. All the players took it for granted, but then again, they had to concentrate on the game. They were the modern-day gladiators people came to watch and cheer. People needed bread and circus entertainment, like the ancient Romans used to prefer.

Some players had their own rituals. One guy always uttered mantras that nobody understood, another one meditated head down to his knees for a couple of minutes, and one guy had an amulet he always kept in his pants. We also had "These Magic Moments" chosen as our theme song played always before we hit the ice. I didn't need any of this since I already had programmed myself for the whole season and eighty-two games. I just tried not to think too much ahead in order to not get frustrated.

The arena was sold out again, and when we entered the ice, the audience went wild. There was this usual scintillating mini-fireworks to spark up the atmosphere. I always insisted to be the last one to enter. Captain and assistants entered first. They wanted to make me another assistant captain, but I declined, stating that I didn't have a big enough hockey resume. Besides, to me, this was only a hobby that I was ordered to do and not a life's passion.

The National Anthem of both Canada and the United States were sung by a famous teen pop group, The Bra Supporters. The visitors were Regina Fur Traders from Saskatchewan, Canada. They had a very good goalie, Rudyard Trapp—by the way, a good name for a fur trader—and without me, they might have called him the best in the league. I felt bad for him because he deserved better, but always all the news media mostly reported of me. I hoped his time would come soon.

I also noticed a sign: "Pro-Con Greets Sherwood." I waved at them and heard a wild noise back.

The game started with the opponent's breakaway. He came from the right, but I already had figured out his first fake attempt and then a shot to the stick side that I could kick away easily. The audience cheered, like having seen a magician's elephant disappear. Well, I felt like I was in a circus, acting as a clown in front of ice-cream-eating kids. There came many more shots, but none of them were dangerous, and they were as easy to stop as they were big beach balls. Because the opponent's goalie, Rudyard Trapp, was good too, we won, only 1–0, but thanks to Angelo McGilliguddy, we didn't need overtime for it since I didn't want to stand there another period like a snowman in the front yard.

After the game, we had the same routines. First, everyone tapped and patted me, and they had the victory rituals, raising their hands and chanting in incorrect English, "Us did it." To me, it was exorbitant. They got used to my reaction already. Then came the media asking the same old questions: "What is the secret of your shutout streak?" "Did you have any hard shots tonight?" "How do you guess where all the shots are aimed at?"

I answered truthfully that I didn't have any secrets and that all the saves were nothing but logic because even the best players always act the certain way. For example, if you leave the other side of the goal open three times, the first two times they try to shoot there and the third one toward me on the other side. Of course, I didn't mention it publicly but kept it as my trade secret.

When I came out of my dressing room, there was an old lady and two family members waiting for me. She was the eighty-eight-year-old passenger I had met on the plane to Helena. I had asked our team staff to invite them to the game and pay for their flights and accommodation. The lady was all smiles and extolled the atmosphere and how good I was. It was so sincere; that was the first time I felt good about being a good goalie. I gave her my autographed jersey and wished them all the best. It sounded like I had lots of personal guests that night in the audience.

*   *   *

In the next game in Omaha, we had a new guy joining us. He had just been called up from the minors, sitting on the other side of the dressing room, but when I heard his first word, I was delighted to realize he was a Finn, not a relative of Huck Finn, but a player from Finland. The word he mentioned was "Perkele" or a stronger expression meaning "Damn it." He had accidentally cut his skate lace with the knife sharp blade.

As soon as I got ready, I went to talk to him, and he was happy to speak his native language. His name was Kaapo Wirtanen, a rare form of the most common last name, Virtanen. We felt like we were relative souls right away. Only we knew that the natives call their country Suomi, and they speak Suomea. Finland and Finnish are only international names of them. I told him about my background and hobby of studying languages. He sounded impressed.

Our chat was cut short though since our coach had last-minute information on the opponent, Never Yielders. I didn't pay attention because I already had decided my long zero goal streak would continue. The hall was sold out already because more than expecting a victory, the audience wanted to see me; that's what the media claimed. I just wanted to communicate with our new substitute teammate, and I hoped he would have a long contract with us.

We won the game, 5–0. It was one of those nights when all went right with us and all went wrong with the Omaha Never Yielders. Nobody seemed to feel really bad since I got a huge applause when I was announced as the second best player after stopping all nineteen shots. To my delight, my fellow Finn had the third star because of his three assists.

After this, our team players were allowed an amazing three days off from practice since we had a big lead in the standings, a rarity in the NHL world. We would fly back to Santa Barbara in the morning, and everyone could spend the night how they liked. Half a dozen of us didn't go anywhere, just watched some TV in the hotel lobby and sipped some martinis, beer, or juices. I had two glasses of cranberry juice.

Next to me sat an old fellow who had lived at the gate of the prairies all through his life. He had been a farmhand, roof maker, and salesman of door-to-door insurance. I was happy he didn't recognize me nor talked about their hockey team. I chatted with him until midnight and then retired to bed. The last guys had come back at three o'clock from a nightclub and had only a four-hour sleep before we had to get up. Well, they had time to recover and sleep some three hours on the plane anyway. Still, I couldn't comprehend this kind of lifestyle.

*   *   *

We arrived at Santa Barbara at noon because of turning clocks back. I drove home with my five-year-old Chevy Cavalier, bought some buckwheat flour, watermelon juice, and cheddar cheese. At home, there was quite a big bunch of mail. Our team was on the cover of *Santa Barbara News and Gossip* again. That meant there had been a slow news week in town. I skipped the sports pages, read the horoscope, glanced through the crossword and the healthy living section, and checked obituaries. I was always intrigued by the memorials of deceased people. I think all humans have their own unique and important story to reflect.

Before our tour, I had ordered a book about old tea-cultivating methods, which was waiting for me. Right after starting to read it and winding down on the sofa, my phone rang. It was Mr. Steele, my agent. His phone call usually meant some kind of inconvenience. He thought he was a big shot, but in my mind, he was a bohemian, inconsiderate brat.

"Are you ready for the mayor's party tonight? Miss California and her two runners-up will be there also. It's a great way to show up and build some VIP connections."

I told him I didn't care about big parties and the least of those artificially made-up, overly self-conscious mannequin girls. I also protested that nobody cared about Druids, those ancient Celts, or medieval church architecture, constellations, or old-time Egyptian embalming methods. They just talked chitchat and gossip about nothing and boasted their fabulous achievements.

Steele claimed that people were already hinting that I was into something else since I didn't have a girlfriend. There was no such thing as a girlfriendless NHL player. I just didn't care because only I knew that I would settle with a right, humble, demure, and pure-hearted lady. Why is it that famous people always attract the most beautiful or handsome partners? But unfortunately again, there was a clause in my contract that I promised to attend important events, so what could I do! Well, Steele had done a nice gesture of ordering some oatmeal porridge for me. That made me feel better. And luckily, I had six hours to spend quiet time first.

After finishing the book, I decided to bake buckwheat loaves according to the new recipe I had cut out of the weekend paper. I mixed flour, spices, water, yeast powder, parsley, nuts, zucchini, and added oatmeal even though it wasn't in the instructions. It took an hour to bake three loaves, and when I took them out of the oven, a delicious aroma filled the room. I was sure even my neighbors, Mr. and Mrs. Braithwaite, could smell it.

I ended up eating the whole loaf at once with cheddar cheese and organic butter on it. I was so proud of my creation that I took one loaf to my neighbors. They were utterly surprised at my gesture. Half an hour later, the lady knocked at my door and gave me half a carrot cake she had baked before and requested the recipe for the buckwheat loaf. The cake was too sweet, but I sliced most of it and froze the pieces for further dessert use.

I decided to wear a traditional Lapland's reindeer herdsman's Sunday costume. The mayor's office was in a 140-year-old building, postbellum so to speak. When I entered, it was already half full of local and Californian dignitaries. The event was to commemorate the construction of the first garrison in the area or something. I wasn't big fan of military, even though I realized it was one of those necessary evils in the world. If we weren't that competitive and selfish, we would not need armies and could feed poor people instead. But the whole world history was history of wars. At least in the olden days, they had more simplistic yet exotic weapons to kill and wound one another.

Mr. Steele dragged me right away toward the center and introduced me to Miss California Penelope Lilly or something like that. She had a low-cut dress and a professionally mellifluous smile that I didn't find attractive, and when she learned who I was, her eyes went wide in admiration. Out of common courtesy, I greeted her neatly.

Miss Lilly asked me about the dress, and when I told my mother's mother was a Sami healer from Finland's Lapland, she asked me to say something in Finnish. So when I uttered, "Anteeksi, mutta onko tassa kaupungissa tahkokauppiasta," she wanted to know what it meant in English. After I translated it to "Excuse me, but are there any grindstone shops in this town?" she excused herself and went away. I shook hands with a couple of more people, mentioned the usuals, and quickly went to the balcony. The night sky looked amazing.

I stood there for ten minutes when Steele and Mayor Kwiatkowski entered.

"You know how ludicrous this hockey schedule is. Oh, here's my protégé, Mr. Sherwood," Steele blurted to him.

After congratulating me for my feats (which actually was only my assigned job) and asking about the costume, he wanted to know how I liked downtown Santa Barbara. I said that it had a beautiful starry sky and lots of history.

"Did you know that when Venus crosses the Square of Pegasus this month, the last time it happened was when Mayans were predicting the future from the Pleiades. Also, it marks the 167th anniversary of the promotion of General Sherman."

The mayor knew Sherman's troops burned down the old Atlanta in the Civil War and thus inspired the book and movie *Gone with the Wind*, one of his favorites. I stated that as a female writer, Margaret Mitchell had to fight to be able to get it published with the fee next to nothing. At that point, my agent proposed to return inside and raise the glass for the successful team. Also, our captain, Adam Chlumskuy, and leading scorer, Jacques Clementine, had emerged there, and they smiled when they saw me. They were wearing black pinstripe suits themselves. Later on, I saw Chlumskuy go all around Miss California. I could only shake my head in disapproval.

After that, we played against our California rival, Sacramento Gold Miners. It was a walkover, and we downed them 3–0 with almost lackluster effort. I think I stopped some forty shots because I was selected the first star the fifteenth time in nineteen games. That was like a full constellation of Dragon already, but who was counting! I realized that during the game, I was thinking more and more about old historical mysteries. My mind wandered from Easter Island to Persepolis and Mohenjo Daro. There's nothing but idle time when the puck is on the other side of the field.

Well, probably the closest call so far was when the opponent sent a volley puck toward me from their side, and it bounced unexpectedly right in front of me. Perhaps there was a crack on the ice that made it veer nastily, but I could handle it. However, I heard a gasp from the audience. Up to this day, it's funny but awesome that not even the other teams' home audiences ever booed for me. I always got an applause or cheering as if I was their goalie. A weird thought occurred to me that actually they came to see my play as much as their own team's. I didn't care since deep inside, this was futile to me.

The next night we, the Eskimos, had a game in Salt Lake City. The Missionaries were third last in the league standings, but they gave us a real fight. After overtime, the game was still 0–0. Then started shootout rounds. They tried every imaginable trick: surprise slap shot from afar, a spinaround backhand, fake shot, and before-mentioned five-hole attempt, but nobody could fool me. Eventually, in the seventh round, Igloomakers' Murray Jamieson scored, and we won.

"The Twentieth Straight Shutout Miracle" headlined our paper at home the following morning. Also, our suburb paper, *Jonesboro Harbinger*, had a half-page picture of me on the cover with the headline, "Sherwood the Magnificent." I guess I must have been secretly delighted at my streak because I even smiled in the press conference, and that picture was captured at that moment. Was I softening with regard to hockey or winning? I hoped not.

* * *

For the next afternoon, they had scheduled a tactics meeting where they watched clips from our games, and coaches analyzed what could have done differently. I was exonerated because it didn't matter to me. I don't know why, but an inner voice told me to go out for a walk. Close by us, there is a three-mile Abernathy Boulevard with a divider in the middle full of decorative plants, shrubs, and trees. It was named after the first town planner who was smart enough to leave a green lifeline in the city.

Some deciduous trees were dropping their leaves already, a sure sign of Southern Californian fall. I spotted a gardener or city sanitation worker raking some leaves there. I admired her toiling and realized that some people worked honestly and hard for their daily bread. It made me feel guilty since I again had made yet an extra million because of my shutout accumulation. During the daytime, the street is quite deserted in the mostly middle-class residential area.

I noticed there were two young guys practicing baseball by doing some short batting and punt shots. They did some easy ones until the other guy, just in jest I guess, slugged it hard. The ball came whistling straight toward the park cleaner. I reacted faster than ever at the goal and caught it with my left hand. I felt pain but luckily didn't break any bones.

"Oh my god, you saved me from getting hurt. I could have lost an eye or something. How did you do it?" she exclaimed.

I told her it was just a lucky shot and threw the ball and some angry words back to the guys.

"You are my hero," she insisted.

I said that many people call me a hero, but I just do things that are supposed to be done.

"So you have had saves before?"

Yes, I had had some saves indeed.

We introduced ourselves; she was Gina, a Brazilian immigrant with a social sciences degree, but she ended up cleaning parks and working on landscapes in Santa Barbara. She had come to the States with her widower father, but he had fallen ill and returned to his homeland some months ago. Gina had a break time at hand, and she insisted on buying me coffee. I told her it was my treat, and I wanted to have green tea instead.

When we entered the Burger Cafe, the teller lady recognized me right away. She knew already I wanted a cup of organic green tea and an oatmeal-bran muffin. To me, oats was perhaps the most perfect ingredient on earth. If they had oats beer, I would probably drink it. Gina was surprised since oatmeal-bran muffin was her favorite too. We had something in common from the very beginning.

At the table, Gina asked if I was regular in the place or how did they know me. The same moment, two teens came with menus in their hand and asked for my autograph. They wished me good luck and another complimented my "great saves" while she stared at me incredulously.

"What kind of saves are they talking about?" she demanded to know.

Hesitantly and a little embarrassed, I confessed I was the Igloomakers' goaltender.

Gina's eyes went wide. She didn't have TV, and she did not read the sports sections. She had heard of me, but she was never into the sports and apologetically mentioned that hockey and any team sports were nothing but vanity to her. I couldn't believe what I had just heard. I felt such an elation in my heart; she was the first person who didn't care about hockey or our team. I replied that I agreed with her 100 percent; hockey was totally a futile game.

"You do!" she stated, mouth agape.

Inside me, I felt that I had met my soulmate and, without having time to hesitate, asked if she would like to become my girlfriend. She said a big yes. After this, she changed the topic and wanted to know what I thought about that boulevard. I said it was marvelous and noticed that she was the first person who didn't want to continue with hockey talk. I blessed my luck.

The following week, we had three home games. I was thinking of Gina continuously, and I went to see her every day to have a lunch together. In an off night, she came to my place, and we cooked together. One night, she surprised me with an oatmeal-cherry pie. It was sinfully good. At this moment, I decided to take the next step and asked her to move with me. She had some Latin temperament, but at the same time, she was extremely sweet. That week, we won Oklahoma City Dust Cloud, 3–0; Manhattan Moneymen, 4–0; and Charleston Landlubbers, 2–0.

One day I told her she didn't have to work anymore unless she wanted. Gina said she would be happy to have only a part-time employment. After the meal, she immediately started to wash the dishes and cleaned the whole counter brighter than it had ever been before. Whatever chore she did, I could sense an extreme effectiveness and excellence. I felt that we were similar since we both wanted to do a perfect job.

Three days later, Gina moved in, and I gave her my credit card to buy something we would need. To my surprise, she was very modest and bought only a dresser, a mirror table unit for the hallway, and a coffee maker and a couple of containers for kitchen. After all, Brazil was the biggest coffee producer in the world. Her frugality impressed me, and I knew I had made the right selection.

*   *   *

After this, we had a routine gig to Boise. We beat Rainbow, 4–0. It was the first time I was only the third star since our rookie Finn had a hat trick and his line mate, Sylvester Dooley, had three assists. So they were the first two stars, and after stopping eighteen shots, I was the third one. We had a game the next night, so we flew back at night, arrived at two thirty in the morning, so all had a day off without practice and I slept until one in the afternoon. I woke up feeling guilty because I knew all the construction guys had to wake up at six o'clock in order to get to work by seven thirty no matter what time they went to bed.

The opponent was our local Californian enemy, Burbank Stuntmen, that we were scheduled to meet four times this season. They obviously had determined to do their everything to beat us; a few times, they blocked my view with three men and there were our defensemen also, but I could sense where the buck was coming and they were quite easy to catch or ward off. We won 2–0, the first goal by Jacques Clementine and other being an empty netter after they pulled out their goalie for a sixth attacker. I was chosen the first star after stopping thirty-seven shots. I felt the team was extremely aggressive, and there were a couple of close calls for me to become run over, but I managed to get out of way in the nick of time after picking up the puck first.

In the postgame interview, there was a new reporter from the local paper, and I sensed he was after some kind of sensation. He questioned my origin whether I was from this planet and also who my real father was. I convinced him I was a regular American guy who lost his privacy along the way and that there were more interesting things in life than this boyish hockey. In my free time, I was immersing in Byzantine church architecture and told him I'd love to be building one with my crane.

"You know those phenomenal-looking facades. They reflect the symmetry of—"

But he didn't want to listen.

My thoughts were with Gina who had come to her first live game. I was wondering how did she feel and if she understood any rules. Meanwhile, the reporter continued wondering why the other goalies would be happy to have a couple of shutouts in the whole season, but to me, it was like a natural thing. I spread my hands in ignorance and said I really didn't know. Somehow he managed to trick me to disclose something I regretted right away. I mentioned that my grandma's mother was a Sami healer, and the next morning I could read from the *Santa Barbara News and Gossip* that I had a witch doctor in my family line. He went to speculate that perhaps I was a sorcerer too.

Gina told me afterward that she liked the game and action very much and that she was proud of my performance. I indulgently warned her not to become too fond of the game. At least, she didn't question where I got my talent. That was the first big league game she had ever attended. Well, it was my twenty-fifth, all because I was pushed and cajoled into this. The only other games for her had been local soccer matches in the outskirts of Sao Paulo. Now she was getting another touch of American lifestyle.

During the two days off, we walked around in the neighborhood and spent a sunny afternoon in the beach, just enjoying the day and each other's company. Gina loved to try new international restaurants, but so far, none of them had anything "oatsy" in their menus. One place, however, promised to get me some, and they went through all the trouble of sending someone to buy quick oats from the store. I really appreciated their effort and tipped them with a $100 bill, which Gina thought was way too much. For her, every penny had always counted.

We had a three-game northeast tour next. In a game against New Haven Bank Robbers, our coach gave our players all the freedom to try solo tricks and unconventional moves. They did, and six goals were scored by six different guys. Usually, if you try something selfish-looking or daring, it would backfire, but now they managed when there was no pressure. To my surprise, I was again the first star, and the rest they said were "drawn out of the hat." New Haven was a lovely city; it had an old Atlantic feel even though it looked mostly modern. The Bank Robbers had been three years in the league but hadn't reached playoffs yet.

A day later, we played in Richmond, Virginia. Coal Hoarders were currently in a five-game winning streak, and we expected an even game. However, our guys had two quick goals and then the game stalemated. Our third goal came as an empty netter when there were three seconds left. Okay, I scored it by catching a puck and quickly hitting it with a stick, and it rolled on its side to the goal, my seventh of a season. The audience cheered as if their team had won. Again, after the game, there were those usual questions and the same answers. I now had twenty-seven shutouts.

In an interview, I explained that the number did not matter otherwise, but mathematically, 27 is 3 enhanced to the third power; it was also the first composite number in the base 10 system that is not divisible by any of its digits. Furthermore, it's the only positive integer not divisible by its digits. Also, numbers 2 and 7 are the twenty-eighth and twenty-ninth numbers in pi, and not many have thought that if you add all the numbers from 2 to 7, it equals 27. In science, 27 is the atomic number of cobalt. Dark matter is thought to make up 27 percent of the universe. In Hindu astrology, there are twenty-seven naksatras or lunar mansions. In the human hand, there are twenty-seven bones, and it's also the international calling code to South Africa. US Highway 27 goes from Fort Wayne, Indiana, all the way to Biscaine Boulevard in Miami, Florida. I sensed the interviewers thought I was crazy; they looked at me dumbfounded, but so be it.

*   *   *

After one day off, we played in New York. We had the whole day and half to kill since the only practice was a half-hour tactic meeting and warm-up before the game. The first day, I went to the Metropolitan Museum of Arts alone since nobody wanted to come with me. I never understood those modern pieces of art and actually wondered how they knew which way they should hang them. If they accidentally hung them upside down or ninety degrees wrong, probably nobody would notice. It's much easier to hang pieces like Leonardo's Mona Lisa in which you cannot err.

The second day, I walked to Hell's Kitchen, a legendarily mysterious suburb in the west side of Mid-Manhattan. It used to be a poorer Irish area, but since it was close to theaters and Actors' Studio, it was also a mix of actors and artists. I really loved old Greek theater and stage plays done in accordance with an ancient model. Later on, Hell's Kitchen had a face lift, and when young people from Wall Street financial circles started to move in, the house prices and rents rose considerably. I had green tea and two oatmeal-cranberry cookies in an idyllic café. I would have sat outside, but there was a cold wind blowing from the river, and I needed to be in fit form for the game.

I took a taxi back to the team hotel and spent two hours in the lobby reading Veda scriptures in modern Sanskrit language. Then it was time to go to our palaver. I took my book to kill time there. Manhattan Moneymen's new arena, the Credit Cardhouse, was at the southwest corner of the Central Park with an unprecedented four-level underground parking for six thousand cars. The arena was sold out for the full season, except for mandatory three hundred seats for visiting opponents' supporters. I noticed the atmosphere was very special, and they said the visiting teams were in awe and only one opponent had won a game there this season.

The game started with huge cheers and roars from the audience. A series of fireworks were shot above both the goaltenders' areas. They looked like little stars in the Andromeda nebula. The game itself went from side to side, like a clock pendulum in quick speed. The first period went. I had faced twelve shots and had one close call, but I could kick it away at the goal line. The second period started again with intensive speed, and during our penalty, I saw three opponents rush toward me. Then it happened: I was reaching the high puck when their biggest guy came straight toward me and tackled me against the post. The goal fell over, and I felt excruciating pain in my right shoulder and my head was spinning. I had fallen on the ice.

For a while, it was quiet, like in a funeral chamber, then I heard a long "oooohh!" from the stands. Next, I realized they lifted me on the stretcher. From the corner of my eye, I saw a pool of blood on the ice and realized my left eyebrow area was bleeding. Someone put a pad on it, and I could not see much anymore. Now there was a huge din in the audience, and people started to applaud, not eagerly, but I guess in sympathy. I was happy with the support that I had always received at any arena.

Soon I heard an ambulance siren, a common sound in a big city, but this time it was for me. I was taken to a hospital and straight to the x-ray room. Our team doctor, Phil O'Mallory, was with them, and he convinced them I would be okay in due course. Next, they took some blood, and after waiting for ten or so minutes, a nurse came and cut my straps, and they took my upper gear off. Someone had taken off my skates and shin pads already, I guess, on my way to hospital. Then I was pushed to another room with tubes attached to my body, and after getting a shot, I don't remember anything.

I woke up at six in the morning with a terrible headache and also pain my shoulder. The nurse told me my dislocated shoulder was operated and torn ligaments fixed and that it would take two to three months to heal. Also, I noticed the team doctor sleeping in the cot in my room. I felt relieved to have a time off from spotlight but felt bad for my team and city and also all the hockey fans. They said that I was the most coveted item in fantasy hockey pools. First, I thought it was a frozen swimming pool, but then someone explained it was a fantasy betting team. I thought it was the biggest vanity, per se, but also felt that I was letting them down. Igloomakers lost the game, 4–0. It was the first game for our backup goalie, Simon Quest.

I flew home two days later. I traveled in first class so that I could sleep comfortably. The stewardesses knew me and had prepared some oatmeal porridge and apricot jam for me. I was so happy that I gave everyone a fan picture with my autograph. When I was pushed out in a wheelchair, my head still bandaged and right hand hanging in support, there were about three dozen newspaper and TV reporters, photographers, and cameramen waiting for me. I was asked how I felt, was it intentional, what was the diagnosis and prognosis, what was I going to do now, etc. I answered that I was in pain and needed a several week's rest and let other people decide if it was intentional or accidental.

In other people's eyes, it seemed to be a total tragedy, like an earthquake or twister had destroyed the downtown. Every day for a full week, the local papers and national sports pages wrote about the incident. The NHL had analyzed the tapes and decided it was done on purpose, and the Moneymen's player, Conan Donnerwetter, was given a ten-game suspension. Many people didn't seem to be happy about it, especially our team staff and Santa Barbara supporters.

Now the common tone was that they had to cope without me and adjust and fight harder than ever. They also believed that goalkeeper Quest would become more confident when gaining NHL experience in the games to come. They lost the first two home games against Indianapolis Polka Dancers and Bakersfield Spiceboys but won the third one, 4–3, over Rhode Island Manatees. Igloomakers still had a huge lead in the standings, and they believed we could make the playoffs.

I had to spend a week in hospital to let it heal well and as soon as possible. During the first three days, they would not let anyone there, except my mother Gina, team doctor O'Mallory, and our director of hockey operations, Mr. Nunn. When I was resting there, I flipped through the TV channels. I realized how many inaccuracies they could have in one Discovery channel show. Then turning back to the local news, there were our TV hockey commentators, Sydney and Ashley, as they were known to the TV audience.

The commentators analyzed the situation and then went back to the draft night and played the tape again. In that one, they were utterly flabbergasted at Igloomakers' first selection: me.

"Are they total rookies even in selecting players?" Sydney complained and Ashley seconded that we could have got Ulysses Po but incomprehensibly overlooked him over an unknown Sherwood. Now they humbly but happily confessed how wrong they had been. I didn't know what to think since I never considered hockey more than a silly hobby.

Exactly at eleven, when visiting hour started, a group of media people rushed into my room. I faced a fusillade of questions: "Do you miss hockey? Do you think it was intentional? What would you like to say to your fans? What are you reading now?"

I replied I didn't miss hockey as a passion, but I embellished a little and said I felt bad I wasn't helping my team. The accident in my opinion was nobody's fault, but it was meant to happen. My message to the fans was that our team needed their support more than ever.

I showed then the Veda scriptures book in Sanskrit language. Someone exhorted me to say something in that Saint script.

"Srathi sarvatha saruatha savathana," I uttered, and all in unison wanted to know what it meant. "Too much harassing," I said first kiddingly. The exact translation was, and still is, "The driver of the chariot is totally watchful."

Next, a lady journalist asked if it was true that I always wore turquoise underpants in the games. I laughed the first time since the accident.

At that moment, Gina appeared with a nurse's uniform on, and she told everyone that that was enough.

"One more question," said someone.

"That's out of the question," Gina told them feistily and told them to come back in two weeks, knowing I would be out of there in another three days.

They left reluctantly, and after thanking her kindly, she was acting so natural. Actually, she looked really great in that uniform, my personal caretaker. She took it off quickly before anyone could have discovered it.

Gina sat there the allowed two hours. We chatted about everything except hockey. I told her about my dream to buy a little tea plantation at the foot of Himalayas when my career was over. She was in favor of my proposition. Actually, I was eager to go there this summer vacation, but I sadly decided to put if off until my career was over. I didn't even want to think how long it would take. But then again, one can never tell what lies ahead of us.

A day later, my agent Steele walked in my recovery room.

"Sherwood, how is your recovery prognosis?" he demanded to know.

"How about 'Good afternoon!' or 'Hello!' first," I retorted.

He said his nonchalant hellos and described how he had a machinery running, and he had booked me a TV talk show appearance, a bachelorette auction, and a visit to the school for the deaf. I promised to do only the last one and told him I wasn't interested in any vanity. Steele insisted that I was a celebrity and I should do all the PR I could. As usual, we had an argument.

Steele also disclosed that in the contract, there was a clause that for every shutout in the playoffs, I would get a $500,000 bonus and he, "a 10 percent reward for his hard work." To me, this was greed, and he was using me for his own purposes. I knew I could get the shutouts, but I let him know I would give that bonus uncut to UNICEF's needy children. Again, grumpily, he tried to explain that I didn't comprehend my value. To him, hockey was big business. My contract was only a one-year trial, but my agent promised to take care of it soon. I ordered him to be modest. Without wishing me a prompt recovery, he left, shaking his head, and I heard him mutter, "Hope they will check up his head too." I felt they should check up his instead.

The other day, Kaapo Wirtanen stopped by and told me about his life in his native Finland. He was born in a small town of forty-five thousand people called Hyvinkaa. Actually the *a*'s in its name had dots for the pronunciation reason. It was more famous for Finnish baseball, a very different version of the American counterpart. It was also the home of Kone elevators. I was glad to talk with him in Finnish and practice all those difficult word bendings and suffixes.

*   *   *

I have been writing this with variegated moods and emotions for two weeks now, sometimes until late night, occasionally only a little in the afternoon. Writing is really a matter of inspiration, not just perspiration. Still, I feel I am a clumsy writer, but I can type much faster now and also think more ahead. I guess I have missed some important points, incidents, and moments, and they might come back only after this is finished. I only hope you would understand my point of view and message here. Now I will make some oatmeal porridge and apricot jam and perhaps continue an hour later.

Actually, it took me two days to resume writing. We decided to go camping for a couple of days, exploring nature. All the places have their own beauty and special characteristics. But what was I going to tell next? Oh yes, I was released home after staying six days in the hospital recovery facility. I made them swear not to tell the media anything about it, and indeed, there were no nosy people waiting outside. Some patients wished me good luck, and I thanked them and gave out some autographs, again all with a different handwriting style.

The following week, I read a few books, just to recover some lost reading time. I loved detective stories and found an unread Agatha Christie. She was a master of hiding the obvious, but halfway through, I knew who the murderer, or actually murderess, was. There were some carefully placed clues along the way, but you had to read them between the lines. The only book where I could not guess the end was Russell Greenan's *The Secret Life of Algernon Pendleton*, a bizarre masterpiece in my mind. I realized my right hand became stiff and sore even while turning pages for a longer time. My healing had hardly commenced.

The following day, my mom invited us for a lunch, but unfortunately, Gina had to go to work to replace an ill person for a couple of days. I knew as a dessert, she would have oatmeal porridge for me. For the entrée, we had baked potatoes and green salad. I wanted to read her a poem I had written the previous night and hear her opinion:

Now cometh all the sorrows, hardships, and twists
And I'll beat them with my bare fists.
My mind might be silky like the night
But my bones are strong and I walk like a knight.
Look at the Lyra star; she's got that smile
It can't be surpassed by Vega, Pluto, or a pile
of other orbiters.
Because the smile, like one of the Druids
Has something permanent like the fluids
That flow in my bloodstained veins.

My mom thought it was original, different, and cool. Gina also had liked it. We ate the dessert in the living room and turned the TV on. There I was again, this time my face on the screen with a headline: "Sherwood, Mystery behind a Man." Next talked a manager of a New York–based laboratory.

"I have invited this press conference because of the discoveries we have made might solve one of the biggest mysteries of our time, namely the origin of Mr. Sherwood."

My mom was astounded, and so was I.

He went to introduce a Manhattan arena worker, Mike Midsummer, who said he had scraped Sherwood's blood out of the ice after his unfortunate accident in game 27 in its twenty-ninth minute. Instead of throwing it away, he took it to a lab to be analyzed, only to repel all the rumors. To me, it sounded just like a Warren Commission, abbreviated WC by the way, on the case of President Kennedy's death.

Lab boss went on to divulge my blood contained a thousand times higher the amount of titanium than regular blood. However, the most curious to him was the fact—their fact, not mine—that it contained traces of rocket fuel and a huge dose of a complex compound called deoxyheksalibidocycline monoprotorate that they use only for one purpose: as a laser light diffuser.

As a backup, I have the newspaper clipping and the whole text word by word.

"So I suggest the following: for some unknown reason, be it he is a space alien or just a twist of nature, the fuel gives him a rocket-like reacting speed, the laser stuff a radar-like observance, and the titanium? It is a little mystery. But as we know, the star Lyra is very high in titanium, our twenty-second element sequence with atomic weight of 47.8. Also, Lyra's conditions, according to the space explorer, indicate that human life is very likely possible there."

As a conclusion, he believed that either my father or mother was an alien from Lyra. My mom said that it wasn't true and why should it be.

This caused a new national sensation. Gina was at my side naturally, but she wondered why I had just mentioned Lyra in my poem like it was more than a coincidence. There had to be a logical explanation. Next, naturally, called my calamity howler Steele, and he invited me for dinner. I knew what it was all about and reluctantly agreed. He ordered a big steak, mashed potatoes, asparagus, three-egg omelet, garlic bread, and apple pie with wine and beer. I had oatmeal porridge with cranberry sauce since they didn't have apricot, plus East Indian tea.

As soon as the waitress left, Steele demanded to know what was going on. Whatever I tried to explain, he just told me to cut the crap and tell him the truth. Finally, I had had enough. I told him that this was getting too weird, and one more ludicrous hint and I would leave this business and hockey forever. Why must everything a little extraordinary be out of this world? If it made him feel better and more convinced, I could start letting them shoot goals. I wasn't that proud of my goalless streak in a little boy's hobby. I was also nothing but a normal layman person. My only explanation was that the blood specimen was somehow tampered. That made him calm down and turn apologetic, and he promised to find out and to do some damage control.

"Is Sherwood from Another Planet?" was the headline in our suburb paper, *Jonesboro Harbinger*. They even had interviewed the NHL commissioner who stated that you can draft a player from any place in the universe. There was nothing in the rules to hinder that. He didn't want to speculate where I was from but reminded that hockey needed stars to make the sports more attractive and extolled my contributions. The TV ratings were up 20 percent, especially nationally televised Igloomakers' games. Much less attention was given to the fact that they lost to Omaha Never Yielders, 4–2, in Nebraska and had only one victory since my sick leave. They still had a lead in the standings, although now Montana had the same points but much more goals allowed.

I noticed that Gina was more quiet and pensive that night. What had impressed me she was never in a bad mood, was always supportive, and did happily all the chores in my house. I kept wondering how lucky I was by stopping that baseball that day in the boulevard. I let her be; after all, she was a woman, and sometimes they could be mysterious. I sat in a La-Z-Boy and thought about all this. I went through all the games, how I had had some impossible saves, how I had become famous and a celebrated star without my will. I never got accustomed to it and perhaps never would.

Then I was thinking of my childhood pal, Bob. I wondered where would he be now. Then it hit me: once we were doing some chemical experiments and made a random concoction of ingredients. In school chemistry, we learned how a color changes when we add certain elements and compounds into a tube. Sometimes it starts to ferment or emanates a strong odor or turns warmer. It is because those ingredients react with one another. What if we made an elixir that I accidentally drank and it gave me all the hockey goalie traits and skills? But two schoolboys . . . I don't know. I remember that after tasting it, I felt funny, but we didn't have titanium for sure, and regular oatmeal doesn't contain it either.

I never thought I would go to a sporting event voluntarily, but Gina wanted me to accompany her to see our Eskimos game in the Igloo. She wanted me to explain some rules and strategies. Actually, I still didn't know them, I only knew my own rule to keep my goal clear. So we went to see Igloomakers versus Toledo Non-Smokers that night. Because the arena was only one mile away, she insisted we walked there. That way, we avoided standing in car lines.

We were sitting on the upper echelons where the press and team president and invited guests sat. The arena looked very different from our bird's-eye view. At times, it reminded me of fast chess, even though in chess, you cannot back up with pawns. It was actually fun because Gina was with me. We lost, 3–5, and I could see all the errors and wrong movements that both goalies made. Simon Quest had guarded the goal ever since I was injured. I felt for him but knew one day he would be better, especially when our defense gathered themselves up. They asked me to train him, but I believed after following my maneuvers during the past twenty-seven games, he should have learned it all. But the thing is, you cannot teach inner hunches and gut feelings, they just occur.

*　　*　　*

When we got home, Gina seemed to be in a good mood. After the blood analysis incident and claims of me being an alien, I had sensed something gnawed at her mind. She was texting her friends and I was watching the History Channel when my phone rang. It was my agent again. The first time since I was drafted, I picked up the phone enthusiastically. He spoke as bluntly as always and just informed me

JONATHAN RIIKONEN

that the whole case was solved totally and infinitely. He was having a press conference next day at noon and told me to watch the news.

I went to bed elatedly but somehow on the alert since after all, Steele was a cunning man. Gina made omelets for breakfast, and for a change, it was actually delicious. I only hoped I would not ail from oatmeal deficiency. I spent the whole morning inside, trying to read science magazines and Gabriel Garcia Marquez's book, *One Hundred Years of Solitude*, in Basque language while Gina was shopping for some new clothes. I realized she had started to spend more and more money, but I didn't care. Steele had just got my face in a protein shake bottle, don't remember which one, for a million dollars' compensation. It was supposed to hit supermarkets within two weeks or so.

Finally, at noon, the local news started. Gina had also arrived and sat next to me. The first flash in the screen was Mr. Steele's face. He had worked hard to make himself famous, and at least in Santa Barbara and hockey circles, he was well recognized, a household name so to speak. After a couple of other upcoming stories, a house fire, and the city planner's project, the picture went back to Steele. He wore a dark blue suit and a too-wide-looking tie. Again, this is from the newspaper clipping, so this is an exact copy of what he was saying:

"Ladies and gentlemen, I am here today to cleanse the smeared reputation of my client, Mr. Sherwood. First of all, his family tree has its roots on this planet. All these allegations have been much ado about nothing, causing needless and indescribable stress and embarrassment to him and his closest ones."

He went on telling how he hired two unbiased investigators who didn't leave a stone unturned, and this is what they found:

"The blood that was scraped from the ice was not anyone else's but, indeed, Sherwood's own." People in the room sighed loudly. "But it was scraped from the painted red goal line. And paint's one main material is titanium, which explains that rare metal content. Before every game, they turn the lights down and have fireworks, which, surprise, contain little agents of high octane petroleum we refer to as rocket fuel. And one bazooka is right above the goalie line, scintillating tiny particles down. And then this laser compound I won't even try to pronounce. This Mr. Midsummer had just serviced the laser scanners of ticket machines, adding some liquid into the system with his bare hands. With the same hands, he picked up the scrapings and pieces of paint and deposited them in the container," my agent explained.

The media people were dumbfounded, only because they didn't discover a news sensation. After all, I was declared a normal citizen. Then Steele wrapped this up, stating, "As you all see, this conspiracy happened because of a careless handler, an overcurious and stupidly smart arena worker who wanted to become famous. I believe he will be fired immediately. And as for Sherwood's return, it's about two weeks away. Thank you and have a good day!"

Then he walked away, and commentators started to analyze the whole thing.

Relieved, I mentioned to Gina how awesome he was. She looked at me incredulously and suggested we had planned this explanation together at that dinner.

"You have always said that Mr. Steele is a very ruthless man, and now, all of a sudden, you praise his eloquence," she retorted and reminded me of my poem about Lyra and everything.

She rose and said she deserves to know the truth. What could I say? I was not an alien but a normal American guy who only had an extraordinary talent.

"And you don't wanna have money. Don't you understand how lucky you are? I wanted to become a teacher in Sao Paulo, but I never

JONATHAN RIIKONEN

had a chance, so I ended up sweeping streets here, only dreaming about a house on the hills," she retorted with tears in her eyes.

She reminded me there was always ways to handle big money. Set up a foundation or something for underprivileged children, but I had overlooked it. Then Gina left for a walk and slammed the door after her. I had never seen her like this before. I sat on the sofa a long time dumbfounded. Yes, I could accept the money, I guess. So I rushed after her.

I knew she would head for the Almaden Park as always and spotted her there walking toward me. I didn't know what to say next, but I didn't have to. Gina jumped into me, embraced, and said how happy she should be that I, a celebrated star, picked her, a nobody. Again, I convinced her that she meant more to me than a roomful of *Sports Illustrated* swimsuit models. I felt she had always understood my pain and yearning for privacy.

Then a bird was frolicking in the air and suddenly put out a dropping. It was falling straight down on Gina. Instinctively, I stretched my arm to pick it from midair and realized it didn't really hurt anymore. I was obviously healing, but still, I could not carry heavier things like shopping bags or library books. That evening, the Braithwaites invited us over for a cup of tea, and we gladly accepted. We brought them a pack of dozen oatmeal-pumpkin-wheat bran cookies from the mall's bakery. We had good time after they could also verify that I was just a regular mortal person and not an alien.

*   *   *

Igloomakers had a hard time in their road trip. The Eskimos lost to Little Rock Roosters, 0–4; Tallahassee Turtles, 1–3; and to Pumpkins, 2–5, in Baton Rouge, Louisiana. They were still at the playoff run, but how long? The press wrote despairing articles, one was headlined

"SOS, Sherwood Needed!" and another one: "Doomsday Approaching Soon: Santa Barbara Losing the Playoff Race." I had mixed feelings about that, but I certainly hoped it would not distract our acting goalie. Unfortunately, for townspeople, ice hockey was evidently much more than just a harmless hobby.

As every week, I had to go to see the team doctor, O'Mallery, in order to evaluate my healing development. My shoulder was stretched to many ultimate positions, and they asked when it hurt. I guess everyone's muscles hurt if you twist them enough. They took six x-rays from different angles, and I was declared healthy. Now I was ordered to do stretching exercises and intake lots of magnesium and other natural products.

In a week, I was supposed to go back on ice and attend the first practice since the second day in their training camp. Of course, I didn't do anything except when greeting someone, opening doors, picking up stuff from shelves, scratching my back, or turning pages in books. I just found it senseless to do exercise for the sake of exercise. That night, we watched together the last two periods of our home game.

Eskimos had Madison Antelopes visiting, and the first time, there were some empty seats in the stands. That proved to be a high shooting game, and even though the goalies did some amazing saves, it was 3–3 after the regulation. Valentino Matuschanaskavasky had scored twice and Al Moonglow the third one. So it went to a five-minute overtime with only four skaters on each side. Only a minute and half into it, the opponent scored, and we had another devastating loss. Now we had fallen out of the playoffs race. However, they announced that after a three-game road trip, I would be returning, and they gave a huge applause. I felt a little uneasy. The spotlight was waiting,

That night was amazingly clear, and we went for a late-night walk. I introduced Gina to the different constellations and their role in the celestial universe. I explained how a square of Pegasus was so important to ancient Aztecs. When the planet Venus entered it every seven years, they sacrificed seven seven-year-old children to ensure good weather and crops in the next span. Gina was curious whether there was life in Pegasus, and before I had a chance to answer, she inquired if I believed in UFOs. I knew we were past this alien fuss in the media already, and I could sense innocence in her manner.

I answered that it was a very ambiguous question. She demanded to know why, and I said the same thing that I would always tell to anybody. "Because it is not a matter of believing but acknowledging your own mind-set. Think of an earthworm: does he know that people exist? No. They live in their own little circles. But us, we know the worms. It's just a matter of juxtapositioning or counterjuxtapositioning your stand toward, you know, the thing."

She didn't know what to say next, but suddenly, there was a shooting star. It appeared out of nowhere, and a second later was gone. I said that NHL is full of puck shooting stars, and she added also goalies that catch them.

Then I got an idea. I wanted to surprise Gina. Why hadn't I realized this before? Pro-Con was constructing a new twelve-floor apartment building nearby where there used to be a junkyard with a few homeless people's shacks. I had bought and donated them an old building, and now they were modernizing the site. We walked there. I still knew the gate's electronic code and opened it. As well, I knew where they kept the crane key and picked it up.

Next, we found us climbing up the crane. When approaching, Gina was getting scared, but I told her not to look down yet. We entered the cabin, and I realized that was the same crane I had operated for over three years. The tears almost spilled on my cheeks. I let Gina sit in the seat and showed her what to do. She pulled one lever, and the crane made a full turn. Santa Barbara looked so beautiful in night lighting.

For Gina, it was like being in a carousel, and she felt like she was young again. I told her that we all are forever young since only the universe is old.

"You always find a philosophical point of view even when rotating a crane boom," she commented.

Then she spotted an ambulance down there. Perhaps either somebody was dying or someone was giving an emergency birth. One could see the entire spectrum of life from up there.

*   *   *

Toward the end of week, it seemed like the media was mostly talking about my return. Our team lost to Cheyenne Beehives, 1–3; to Montana Scarecrows again, 2–5; and to our other local rival Bakersfield Spiceboys, 0–2. A day after they returned, I was taken to the practice again. They tested me hard, and sometimes I faced two pucks at the same time, and three times I had to pick one from behind my back. The common feel was that I was ready, and they announced my return in the evening news and morning paper. We had a four-game home streak in the following seven days.

In the game night, when I entered the arena, the audience gave me a standing ovation. The visitor Kentucky Ice Derby had their own hundred or so loyal fans behind their team bench with streamers and team jerseys. The game started, and I warded off a few easy shots. Six minutes into it, Adam Chlumskuy scored and turned our spectators wild. After this, the game went from end to end, like sea waves on the sand. Then the rookie player, Ulysses Po, had a runaway, and instead of trying to feint or bluff me, he had a huge slap shot. I extended my hand, but it slipped into the goal.

The arena turned totally quiet. For a fleeting moment, there were sounds of sighs in the air and all, except for me, were astounded. Then Po lifted his hands, and Ice Derby players and supporters started to celebrate noisily. For a while, there was a big din in the stands. Even the announcer congratulated Ulysses Po for making a kind of NHL history. He was the first player ever to score against me, and consequently, he ended my record-breaking shutout streak. I felt relieved; they didn't have to talk about it anymore. So I thought, but actually now, they were speculating if I had descended from the high echelons to the level of mortal goaltenders.

Later on, I allowed another goal in a three-man rush. I should have seen and caught it, but somehow I was temporary out of a position, and that's all it takes. Luckily, Igloomakers scored twice after this, and we won, 3–2. We walked out of the ice with "Sherwood! Sherwood!" shouts. To my surprise, I was selected the third star, and I knew it was just to spur me on. On my way back to dressing room, I spotted my grave-faced agent farther in the premises. I walked by as if not having seen him.

In the postgame media meeting, all the cameras were on me. They wanted to know what happened, and I blurted that I guess I missed two pucks. They wondered if I had lost the touch or my hand hadn't healed well enough. I just responded that I felt all right, but that people should quit thinking that I was like Norse god Odin at the gate of Valhalla. I reminded that Parthenon was to last forever but has badly declined. They hyped about playoffs and Stanley Cup chances, and I said anything was possible if I stayed healthy, but it was still a long shot because we had thirty games left.

We had a day off, and then the next morning I was ordered to attend the light practice again. Now I stopped every shot, and Coach Huggenmuellerstrom seemed very contented. Our opponent, Quebec

City Franchophones, had played better than expected and had already beaten two teams in their Western tour. Our arena was sold out, and one could almost touch the atmosphere with a bare hand. The game had barely started when the Francophones had a neat series of passings, and then Pierre Dupont scored a bouncy puck from between my legs. The audience reacted strongly. I could hear oh-nos and my-goshes from many mouths.

Then I decided that this was it; I promised myself this was the last goal I would allow this season. We bounced back quickly and had a one goal lead after the first period by Brad Lee and Nick Nantucket. In the second period, I faced a fusillade of shots, but I stayed alert and picked all of them. In the third, our team added two goals, and we won, 4–1. I was selected the number 1 star after stopping forty-seven of forty-eight shots. Again, the press wanted to know what happened, and I quipped it happened because I was not an alien from another planet but just a regular fella. That was the final period for the alien episode. Thinking about it now, I guess I let it happen subconsciously; I wanted those goals to occur to prove a point.

We had the second part of a double header a day later when Albuquerque Cactus Huggers came to town. Their most followed player was probably Anton Ruby, a six-foot-eight tower for a player. He reminded me of a crane, and that's how I nicknamed him. After mentioning it in a postgame interview, the name stuck right away, and to this day, he's been Crane Ruby. Don't know if he likes it, but nicknames are often given, not chosen.

The third game against Bakersfield Spiceboys was typical me, I should say, since I had no trouble with any shots. I stopped thirty of them with my variety of styles and movements. Again, I could predict where all the pucks would come. We won 4–0, and the next day the local paper headline read, "Sherwood in Top Shape, Playoff

JONATHAN RIIKONEN

Hopes High Again." I never read further than that, but still, what a difference a day makes!

*   *   *

I knew that my mom had always dreamed about a swimming pool. So the next day, when we visited her, I went to the garden to secretly estimate the measurements. I also decided she would get a slide since she once nostalgically said that she had always dreamed about it. I think we all have a little child inside us if we just dare to take a good look. I also wanted to have a sprinkler system installed in her garden, but she refused, claiming it was pure fun to water them. She had never really traveled much, but now I hoped she would start doing it.

My mom liked Gina a lot, and they seemed to get along well. They both had a simpler background and the same kind of humor and caring nature united them. They had been shopping a couple times and sometimes baked goodies together. I always got oatmeal cookies. More than once, I was asked why I liked oatmeal so much, and I usually replied that I suffered from oatmeal deficiency. Why did some others like garlic or potato pancakes or cherry wine? It's because we are made of different elements. I had never had a beer in my life and only a few times half a glass of wine. Alcohol did not make me happy, only thirsty for water.

Next, it was our turn to visit local rival, Bakersfield. I was again exonerated from the practices because I had another zero game, and I enjoyed my free time greatly. I hoped I should never go to training again. We went there by bus, so we had to leave at noon. We had our palaver on the bus, and after a break at the gas station in Castaic, we could take an afternoon nap. I wasn't really into naps, they made me feel drowsier. I watched the movie and listened to it via headphones. When in Bakersfield, we had dinner first. When finished, it was two and half hours before the H-hour, just enough time to digest it well enough. I had mashed potatoes, broccoli, fish, and a cup of tea with a piece of cheesecake.

Even before the season started, we were coined as local rivals with Spiceboys. We had won them already once, and this time we beat them, 6–0. Our coach again allowed us laissez-faire mentality, or everybody could try their personal tricks and strengths. It worked out again, and I just did my part by keeping the goal line unsurpassed. Now the third lineup guy, Leonardo Greenstreet, scored twice and added an assist and was chosen the first star. I was so happy for him since an almost forgotten guy got some accolades. The spectators didn't seem to care if they lost since I guess they were expecting it. I got several applauses when I stretched my best to stop the pucks.

We spent the night in an old but restored Roosevelt Hotel and had a breakfast call at nine. I had become Kaapo Wirtanen's roommate. I loved to chat with him in Finnish, one of the most complicated languages that exist. I learned a new thing, namely that almost half of the last names there end with "-nen," which actually is a diminutive form of a substantive. So Wirtanen meant in old Finnish "Little Stream." Now it would begin with V. An hour later, we were back on the bus and on our way home. The very next day we would fly to Ohio to play against Akron Rubbernecks. The team name naturally reflected the Goodyear factory that dominated the labor market there.

We had a sold-out house, and there were lots of noise in the air. Again, I heard my name chanted from the crowd. We had an honorary face-off featuring two war veterans as part of their theme night. Those just delayed the game, but I was happy ordinary people got some attention, not just rich and mighty puck chasers. I have sometimes wondered what if they made me a forward instead. Would I have scored a lot since I know where those puck should be shot, and would

JONATHAN RIIKONEN

I have been able to outmaneuver the opponents and give great passes? Skating looks like hard work, and I would not like to practice often, or maybe they would let me rest if I scored a goal or two in every game. But at least I didn't need to be that fit in goal; for me, it was just mostly standing idle.

We ended up winning, 3–0, I think, but who cares. I guess at least hockey pool enthusiasts do. I heard that many people compete against one another by picking players in turn and forming a team. They count the points, goalie shutouts, and goons' penalty minutes, and the winner is whose players accumulate the most points. Can you imagine that normal levelheaded adult-aged people doing this? So my shutout probably generated many poolers lots of points. When I was on sick leave, I must have let them down, but then again, given other pool goalie owners a fairer chance.

Because of the crazy hockey scheduling, we had to fly home at eight in the morning when it was Saturday and only six o'clock in Santa Barbara. We had the game the same night at six, twelve hours later, a thing that really shouldn't have happened. At least after that, there were three off-days before the next home game. Our weeknight games always started at seven thirty, but this one was more comfortable for the East Coast TV audience. Our games were rated nationally number 1 for who knows what reason.

We arrived home a little before noon. So our diligent crew took care of our gear, and we were sent home to sleep an extra couple of hours. Even I was ready to go to bed, the first afternoon nap this season. Gina woke me up at two thirty. She had made me a big plateful of oatmeal porridge that I had missed already during our road trip. We met at the arena at four thirty, had a quick briefing, and we went to the dressing room. The opponents loaded their stuff from the bus the same time. It takes close to half an hour to get the goalie paraphernalia on.

It was my first meet with Austin Stetsons, a Texas team that they had already visited during my dismissal. They were the only major league team ever to have triplets in their team: Gregory, Timothy, and Zachary Bixby. Gregory and Timothy were forwards playing in the same lineup and Zachary, a defenseman. I was contented that now the crowd had something else to follow and wonder, not just only me. The Bixby brothers were gentlemanly players, and nobody had any penalties yet. It was already discussed that they should grant Lady Bing trophy collectively to all three of them. Anyway, whatever they tried to do, I had to stop all the attempts. So we won, 5–0, and we were rising in the stats.

*   *   *

There was an elated feeling in the dressing room that night. A wearing and exhausting stint was behind us, and we were given two days off. So after the game, everyone agreed to go to the bar, and the team did not set any limits what it came to beer or spirits. Usually, it's two beers or a small glass of something stronger. I was very hesitant to go. I wasn't tired, rather I just needed my own time. But it was the Finn who cajoled me to join them. He said it's their tradition that you booze if you lose and double treat if you win. Thus, I decided to try it once in my lifetime. I had never really had any alcohol, once or twice a thimbleful of red wine, and that's all. I called Gina to come and pick me up at ten thirty.

We went to the bar just across the street from the western side of the arena. It was teeming with people, and we got an applause when we entered there. However, they soon concentrated on their own business, except for some younger women who were all over our teammates. After all, half of them were more or less single anyway.

"What is your favorite poison?" asked a player next to me.

I replied honestly that it was green tea, which made the others laugh. "A joke, right?" commented someone.

Before I realized, they brought me a glass of greenish drink that even smelled funny. They urged me to drink it. It didn't taste good but not bad either, rather I'd say strange. I don't remember much after that, but the time seemed to pass fast. I think someone brought me another one; at least, I didn't order or pay any. I was getting tipsy when one girl came to taste my drink and sat on my lap. Even though I tried to resist and push away, she would not go. I turned my head to listen to Finn, and when I turned back, this companion suddenly kissed me on the mouth. It was a long and wet kiss and made me feel awkward, but that was only the prelude of it.

At that very moment, Gina walked into the bar. Her eyes went wide, and the girl jumped out of my lap. I couldn't even stand up. Why did these guys have to do this to me?

"I can't believe this," Gina exclaimed.

She was gone as quickly as she had materialized there. For a while, I sat there mesmerized. This had a huge sobering effect on me. I rose and rushed after her but didn't see her. I started to walk home, and it took me twenty minutes to reach there. I went in, but it was dark and nobody was there. I saw a light inside the Braithwaites and rushed there and knocked on the door. The lady opened the door in her bathrobe, gave me an aghast stare, and told me that Gina had packed her stuff hurriedly and said she was heading to Austin to her aunt and left for the airport.

Now I didn't have time to waste. I called an Uber, and it came in ten minutes, which felt like an hour. I ordered the lady driver to step on it, and off we went. Luckily, the airport is quite small, so I knew where to find her. She was shopping a ticket at the last-minute booking counter. I ran toward her and shouted from halfway, "Gina, what are you doing? Where are you going?"

This caused a big ado since people realized who I was. They were praising our good game and success and my feats. I only nodded in haste. Gina said she was going away for a while; she saw me kiss that woman. I claimed it was her who kissed me since I had never been drunk before or after this either.

"Looks like you do nothing like a normal person, nothing!" she yelled back.

Now we were surrounded by a crowd of passengers and their attendants. The men seemed to back me and women, to support Gina. Talk about male and female bonding!

"You don't have to take this, Gina!" proclaimed one lady, and others urged her to go away also.

"You don't have to take this either. You are a young guy and can get any woman," a guy exclaimed, and others seconded.

But I wasn't interested in anyone else, and besides, I felt I could not win without her. Gina claimed that I could before her and called me a penny-pincher. In despair, I promised her we'd get a house on the hill.

"House on the hill!" repeated the crown in unison.

Yes, and Santa Barbara needed me since we had got the city into the headlines and given the town a big moral boost. I knew that even it was only a child's play game. I promised I would never do such a foolish thing again. This made Gina melt, and she came close to me and hugged me. The audience gave us a big applause, and all of a sudden, I felt so embarrassed. We walked out among good-luck shouts and cheers.

On our way back, I felt hungry, and we decided to stop at McDonald's where I hadn't dined since I met Gina in that boulevard. Gina took fries and a salad and when contemplating, I realized there was an item called McSherwood. I asked what that was, and the attendant told me it was oatmeal with apricot jam and green tea. I took one elatedly. Behind me, there was a family with three kids, and they enthusiastically ordered the same.

I noticed all of them were wearing the Eskimos' pink jerseys. Obviously, they were coming from the game either in a traffic jam or walked all the way there. I heard the cashier order five more McSherwoods from the cooks. I took my autographed cards and gave them all one. Only then they realized who I was, their eyes went wide and mouths were like those smiley icons.

*   *   *

The basic season was nearing the end. We had one more home game and then a two-game road trip before the playoffs. If we won them all, we would get a home-court advantage in the playoffs, not that it really mattered to me. Three days later, we played our last home game in the regular season. It was April 1, also known to many as April Fool's Day. Who were we kidding by playing hockey when it felt like summer already? Our visiting team was Oklahoma City Dust Cloud. Someone had once said that Montana was America's biggest truck stop, Idaho the biggest potato field, Arkansas the biggest chicken hatch, and Oklahoma the country's biggest dust cloud. So it had become a catchphrase, and when a team from Detroit moved there eight years ago, it was renamed the Dust Cloud.

Their leading scorer, Sylvester Yeoman, had forty-nine goals already, and he tried to break the magic fifty barrier. He was so determined that I was especially warned about him. The game went routinely, and despite facing seven shots from him, I managed to keep my record untouched, well, minus those two games and three goals earlier. Now I kind of regretted having let those goals, although it was vanity even to think about them. Still, hockey was only hockey to me, not life or a big achievement.

We went to win, 2–0; it was one of those games that didn't impress much, but we all did our job. I felt bad for Yeoman, but at least, he had two more games left. Gina came to watch and gave me some compliments. I guess that episode before had left a mark on her. I knew now it would never happen again, and we would live happily ever after. I just knew. The following morning, I was lazing around and reading a book in Aramaean language. Gina was doing this and that and fed me with oven-made potatoes, broccoli, oatmeal muffins, and tea.

We had to leave for the airport at midafternoon. We flew to Indianapolis to play against Polka Dancers. Some guys were eagerly talking about the Indy cars and other nonsense. I never understood what the big deal was. A car is vehicle to go from place A to place B. Hockey was quite new there; this was their third year, but the town had adopted their team well. It was not sold out, but the fans seemed to be enthusiastic. They were out of the playoff race already, so basically, they had nothing to lose, except that they did, 0–3. I had almost forgotten that I could score when they had an empty netter. So that was my ninth or tenth goal, I could check it out from the paper later.

Our hotel was nice, and we were told to go to bed early to fly to Concord, New Hampshire, via Cincinnati. Their team was Vermont Splendid Autumn, referring to the colorful leaves. We arrived late afternoon because of the time change. I had never been to New England before this hockey tour thing, so at least, it gave me something that I could cherish. Now it was a metamorphosis time between winter and spring.

The game itself was mostly like a suburb fistfight. More penalties were given than in any our games before, and it looked like the referees and linesmen had lost their touch. Among those cleaner moments, we scored four times. However, since Elvis Lives team Memphis also lost, Vermont was the last team to qualify to the Eastern conference playoffs. After the game, we all got a big applause.

Now the teams had played eighty-two games, but I played only fifty-seven. If we did well in the best-of-seven playoffs series, where four victories made a team to advance, that meant three-by-four games in our conference and then four more in the finals. That's what I calculated anyway, subconsciously knowing that things don't always go as they are supposed to.

We had five days off to rest and prepare for the first Stanley Cup playoffs round. Meanwhile, the media did not rest, but they were already in full hype. All seemed to be sure we would have a total sweep in the series. My name Sherwood was mentioned so many times that even a toddler would know it. One day I drove to the desert with Gina, I guess to escape all the hullabaloo. It was amazingly a warm day there. We sat in the car at the roadside stop. I played my favorite baroque music tunes, stared the desert bushes in the breeze, and talked about this and that. We made a long walk and discovered how many little animals actually live there. What if I stepped on the rattle snake? That would be perilous for our team.

We were returning back to the car when my phone rang ominously. I noticed it was my agent Steele. As always, he didn't waste time for little courtesies but went straight to the point.

"Sherwood, I have got fabulous news. I have worked my butt off for your new contract and—"

I didn't even know that I needed a new contract and told him so. I still hadn't read my earlier contract that had brought me already almost ten million in salary and bonuses and from promotion deals. Steele said he was approaching an unprecedented but well-deserved deal. I argued that I was happy already with my huge money, but he claimed this was big business and I was entitled to my fair share. Of what? By stopping rubber pucks like a clown while some others were doing honest work, like building buildings!

My agent stressed that if I only had shutouts in the finals and brought the Cup to town, only the sky was the limit. I blurted out shutouts were no problem and then tried to convince him that all the people are as valuable, and Gina nodded next to me. She had finally understood my pain and principles. Steele advised me to "forget all that humanity crap and grow up."

After another slate of arguments, he disclosed we were close to a four-year and $100 million deal, and his cut would be a "modest" $5 million. He was so excited that I felt he could have kissed me.

"Why don't they lower ticket prices instead?" I wondered.

"Listen to me, you hardheaded hockey hero. You can buy your own crane or whatever—"

Lucky me, at that moment, my phone went blank since I had run out of power. I shook my head, and we headed home and never touched the topic that day again.

In the morning, my mom called. She had received an unexpected visitor, my agent. First, she thought that I hadn't paid for his services. Steele said that was not the case. He went to convince her that I should happily sign the contract. She had retorted that she didn't run my life and also explained that I had always been modest. Next, Steele went on to say that without him, Sherwood would not be making a penny in hockey. My mom said it was just the opposite: without me, Steele would not have made a penny here.

Steele reminded her that sports is a big business, and everyone should get as a big piece as possible out of it.

"Don't you understand how unhappy Sherwood is with all this hoopla? He only plays for his city because he has a big heart. He doesn't have any other motives."

That said, she sent my agent out. What a smart lady! To my relief, our sign-up press conference would only happen after the season was over.

*   *   *

Our first opponent was Boise Rainbow from the spud state, Idaho. They were the only team with seven colors in their attire; thus, they didn't even need a second one. In hockey, if the jerseys and pants of opposing teams look too similar, it's the visitor who must wear something alternative. In this case, we were dressed in full pink anyway. Igloomakers were above them in the standings, so we started at home.

I could feel the atmosphere like in our first three home games. All were excited, and there was more noise than perhaps ever. Rainbow was a good defensive team, so we commonly expected a low score meet. Perhaps the support of the crowd helped us relax, boosting us to beat them, 3–0. I faced only eighteen shots and wasn't even sweaty after the game. In the dressing room, the mood was elated. Nobody dared to mention the Stanley Cup aloud since they believe it brings bad luck. To me, it was only a container made of metal, somehow coveted by some like an alchemist's wisdom stone in ancient times.

Two days later, we had another home game before moving to Idaho. It was almost a copy of the first one. Again, we won, 3–0, and I now stopped twenty shots. When needed not to be alert, I looked around and spotted my agent sitting up there with a glass in hand. He was my so-called hardworking agent. Toward the end, I tried my old trick or sent the puck in a volley toward the opponent's goalie. He realized it the last moment, but this time it only bounced into the crossbar, and we could hear the clink sound well. Audience went a big "ooooh!" Angelo McGillicuddy, Leonardo Greenstreet, and Valeri Vikulov scored for us. Since it was McGillicuddy's thirtieth of the season, he was named the first star.

When we landed in Boise Airport, the rain had just abated, and the sun was becoming visible again. It formed a beautiful, almost fairy-tale-like rainbow. What a coincidence; to arrive to play against the Rainbow, and here it was, greeting us already. They had naturally a full house there even though seriously, nobody believed they could beat us.

We won the game, 4–0. In the press meeting, our coach Huggenmuellerstrom disclosed their plan: our backup goalie Simon Quest would always play the fourth game if we led the series, 3–0. That way, he could get some valuable playoff experience, and if we lost, we could play a decisive game number 5 at home. And yes, we lost 2–4 to the delight of Idahoans. I brought a book to kill time at the corner of the player's box. I have no idea how the game went, only checked the end result from the board.

Our next home game was a 5–0 walkover, and now we had to wait for our second round opponent. After the game, when we walked out of the dressing room, I heard a familiar voice call my name. I turned around, and here he was, my youth pal, Bob, with whom I did some chemical experiments. He had changed a lot from those days, but so had I.

"The last thing I would have expected is that you would become a huge sports star," he said while coming to hug me.

I replied that life doesn't always go as we plan it.

Bobby had married and had two little kids and a farm in Kansas where he was trying some experimental natural fertilizers. So he had followed his dream and was in the chemical field. I said I would be happy to escape to Kansas also, but I had all these contracts and responsibilities now. I invited him for dinner, and while in the restaurant, the first thing he said was "No oatmeal for me please." We had a good time together, talking about our lives, families, and the oddities of human fates. I would have liked to give him free tickets to our next game, but he had to fly back. He promised to watch every game from their satellite TV.

In the next round, we would play against Regina Fur Traders from Saskatchewan. They were the only Canadian team left in the Western conference. We were told nobody wanted to meet us in early rounds, and I guess it was understandable. We started at home again and this time won only 1–0, no matter how hard our guys pushed. The Fur Traders goalie, Sylvester Dooley, stopped forty-three pucks and as a courtesy was chosen as the first star player. I was the second and Eskimos' lone goal scorer, Rex Le Pompadour, the third. Now all the guys had a visible beard because it's one of those things in NHL that nobody shaves until their season is over. I didn't want to do it. I thought I looked silly in a beard. I told the media my beard simply refused to grow. Players never commented on my beardlessness. I guess they didn't want to break the magic.

The other game, we cleared 5–0. I had one really close call, a surprise slap shot from behind our player, but I managed to fend it off via the sidebar from where it bounced out. The audience sighed audibly. Two days later, we headed to Regina. I guess I wasn't thinking since I forgot my passport. We had two options: either try to talk me over or have it sent by FedEx overnight service. To my relief, the customs guy was a big hockey fan and let me come without a problem. He only took my fingerprints and saw them to match. This was the first time I realized my celebrity status helped me out of potential trouble. We decided to play it safe and have Gina send the passport to my hotel since we had to wait one day before the other game. We won, 2–0, and lost the other one with Simon on goal, 1–3.

Just when we thought all was okay for me to return to the United States, the customs official wondered that there was no record of me entering Canada. She didn't know anything about hockey, and it took a phone call and our assistant coach Ek talking to the supervisor before I was freed to come. In the old days, it was easier to enter the States; you just signed up at the New York Harbor and you were a new resident.

Our last Western conference round was against previous year's champions, Montana Scarecrows, and we had to start at their home court. Without us, they would have been considered the biggest favorites, and even now, the most daring ones expected an upsetting surprise. Helena was a nice mountainous town, and I liked its fresh air and friendliness. Unfortunately for them, we were not very friendly visitors since we outscored them, 3–0 and 2–0.

The latest one was a Sunday early matinee game, and we flew home the very same night. It was good to wake up late at home and have two days to recover. The others had only a day off and then a light practice, but I didn't need to attend because I still had kept my goal intact. We had already agreed that I would play both games so that we didn't have to fly back to Montana. They sounded very cocksure we would win. Well, we did; the first game, 6–0, and the second, 2–0.

Now a real Stanley Cup fever had hit Santa Barbara, and it felt like the whole town was breathing hockey. The finals tickets were the hottest items in town. And since we had a four-game sweep and the Eastern conference finals were still unresolved, that meant up to one week's wait. I decided mostly to relax at home, read some books, and watch nature programs on cable TV. Every morning I went for a walk with Gina and talked about anything except for ice hockey. I usually wore dark sunglasses and a Sherlock Holmes hat to hide my identity. We used to stop in a bakery shop and have a cup of tea or she had coffee and some organic cookies.

*   *   *

Two games later, we heard, well, Kaapo Wirtanen called me first and Assistant Coach later to inform, that Montgomery Moonwatchers had beaten Richmond Coal Hoarders in game 6, thus becoming our opponent. The first game was to be three days later on the road since Montgomery finished ahead of us in final standings. We were to fly there two days from now. The next day I felt unusually tired, not physically exhausted, but kind of very sleepy. I wondered what it was since I had slept well and relaxed the whole week and taken it easy. I didn't want to call our team doctor but believed all would be okay. Or was it a lack of exercise my body had got used to, no way.

I went to bed early and woke up late, feeling a little better. Then we went for a walk, and on the newsstand, we saw *Santa Barbara News and Gossip*'s headline "Stanley Cup Fever Bites SB." I told Gina that I felt feverish too. She glanced at me and said I looked pale and blue. I had to sit down, and the last thing I heard was someone say "Is that Sherwood? Is he drunk again?" then I lost my consciousness. Gina was alert, laying me on the bench and calling 911. She told me later a lot of people had gathered around, and she had told them I was only a Sherwood lookalike. I admired her quick wits at the very distressing moment.

I woke up in the hospital only in the morning. I was in tubes, getting fluids from three bottles straight to my veins. I believed it was the next day, but actually, I had slept forty-five hours straight. Meanwhile, the team had to call again a backup for our backup goaltender Quest. He was a nineteen-year-young Lionel Wolff from our minor hockey associate San Diego Pelicans, I learned later. There was a morning paper, and I could only read the headline "Mysterious Illness Sends Sherwood to Hospital" and underneath "Simon Quest Replaces Him in Stanley Cup Opener in Montgomery." My eyes were so swollen that I couldn't read more. At least I knew now where I was and what was going on.

Soon came a doctor with a head nurse. He checked my eyes with a flashlight, tried my pulse and neck glands, listened to my heart, and asked some questions. I could only reply that I didn't feel any pain, only felt sleepy, then yawned long and fell asleep again. Semiconsciously, I could feel the nurse taking a blood sample from me. I knew that our team doctor was with them in Alabama already. Then my bed was moved to somewhere, probably to MRI or I don't know.

I woke up again in the afternoon, a day later. Mr. Steele was standing at my bedside with another older doctor. My agent wanted to know what was wrong with me, and the doctor explained something like "It's a totally mysterious, painless, feverless virus with no symptoms whatsoever, except sleepiness. He's slept virtually three days straight without even eating oatmeal."

Steele demanded to know if everything possible had been done and the doctor said that no aspirin, rose hip extract, ginseng, castor oil, chromium pills, parsnip paste, boron oxide, a long list of others—nothing seemed to work on me.

"Do whatever it takes: change his blood, give him stem cell radiation, pollen pills, acupressure, hypnotize him, give him more of that Lyra titanium. We will desperately need him at least after the next game. We have lost the first two games already."

I pretended to sleep. I simply didn't want to talk with him about the future contract or anything else. Soon I was asleep again until I had a tender shake on my shoulder and I felt moist lips on mine. It was Gina. She brought me some books in Sami and Khmer language and a big box of oatmeal-cranberry cookies; what a thoughtful deed. I had to force myself to stay awake. She sat with me half an hour and told me about the latest personal and national news. I mostly nodded, yawning as a sign that I had got 'em.

After Gina left, the night shift doctor came to make his checkout visit with an assistant or trainee with him. He asked me routinely how I was, and I said I felt like Sleeping Beauty's cousin. At that point, the female doctor-to-be got an idea. In the class, they had just quickly passed the topic of a decaf syndrome. The other doctor was dumbfounded and agreed and said, "I'd be darned. You are probably right, miss!"

It was an extremely rare condition in which one's body metabolism changes through a very complicated chemical reaction. It turns body's noncaffeine content into a deficiency. In other words, I needed to balance myself with thirty times overdose of caffeine, but the body needed a couple of days to adept. Ordinarily, this amount would kill, but in this case, it would turn me normal. Without extra caffeine, it would take up to four weeks to balance. The young doctor told me this happens each year only to one person out of ten million, and I happened to have it right now. They brought me a flat of Coke cans and told me to drink as much as I could. I drank about ten cans and went to sleep.

The next morning a nurse asked me how I felt, and I said I felt like going to bathroom. I was a little stronger or more alert but still could have slept anytime. For my breakfast, I got strong coffee, more Coke cans, and caffeine pills. After this, I read morning paper and learned that our Eskimos had lost both games in Montgomery, 3–5 and 0–3. The third game would be tomorrow night in Santa Barbara. Another surprise waited for me at noon. I was standing already, but the nurse took me to the lobby in a wheelchair in case I would fall asleep. There, a big horde of media—journalists, TV sportscasters, and cameramen—waited for me. I was almost blinded by the multitude of flashlights and deafened by a fusillade of questions.

Then my doctor took control of the event. First, he disclosed all the details of my condition and a prognosis: I should be all right in two to three days. That made people sigh from relief since our fourth and decisive game was three days away. Our team doctor O'Mallory was also seemingly at ease. Next, the assistant coach, Sid Ek, spoke some words and promised the team would fight hard in their third game. I felt a little awkward because it sounded again like they all depended on me.

I had never been to hospital before but already twice now this season. My stay there went fast. I spent time reading and napping and watching some television. I also curiously checked the end of the game on TV. Igloomakers had a good battle, but eventually, they lost, 2–3. At least, nobody blamed our goalkeeper for the loss. The commentators were already waiting for my return like a rising sun. I decided to bring the cup to our town. In the eve of our crucial game 4, I was released. I was still taking caffeine pills but felt good already. Our local TV crews waited outside and asked me the common questions, and I gave encouraging answers. I woke up the game morning at noon. The team folks had already tried to call me twice, but Gina didn't want to wake me up.

Soon after, the phone rang again; it was our anxious director of player operations, Nunn, who did all the major player contacts. I assured I was sound and ready and would come to the team meal and palaver at four. When I entered there, all the players eagerly welcomed me. I could sense some desperation turning into elation. We did the usual rituals: ate, went through the opponent Moonwatchers' strengths and weaknesses, and then prepared for the game. I hadn't put my equipment on for a while, and it felt like a little strange at first, but I got accustomed to it quickly. When it was time to enter the arena, they sent me first.

The arena burst into a cheery noise, and I felt almost embarrassed. I was just an ordinary guy who had been treated like a savior of the world.

*   *   *

As soon as the game started, I felt as comfortably as at home, well, it had been my second home for six months already. The game moved from side to side, end to end. I faced nine shots in the first period, and it was still 0–0. A few minutes into the second, our Murray Jamieson scored, and toward the end, Rex DePompadour added another one. The third period was just playing and fierce effort from Montgomery and I faced eighteen more shots, but nobody scored. Then they pulled a goalie and took an extra attacker. When I gloved a slap shot, I saw my chance and with a stick sent to the opponent's goal and it went in. The noise in the stands was ear-shattering.

My mom called me at ten in the morning. She had woken up because of a noise and went to the window. There was an excavator and two other construction guys working in her backyard. Only when she went to inquire what was going on, she heard that I had ordered her a swimming pool crew. She was so happy, almost like a child getting her candy. I also told they would erect a slide, and that was like an early Christmas present to her. By the time the heat wave hit the town, the pool should be ready. I was looking forward to have a nice swim also, but fate had something else in store for me.

After two meets away and two home games, we had to alternate the visits, and it meant traveling back and forth, well, provided we won the games since Alabama only needed one more victory. The same afternoon, we flew to Montgomery and were given the rest of the day off. I went to see the city with a couple of lesser known players, Chris Reubens and Apollo Woe. Montgomery is first a little hard to absorb, but when walking on the side streets, you get a homey feeling. I saw a little haberdashery store and bought a funny hair decoration to Gina.

On the way to the rink, I saw the Stanley Cup trophy waiting there already. If Montgomery won that night, it would have been theirs. If we won, it would mean another game at home and, if needed, the decisive game again here. The ceremonies seemed very long, but finally, twelve minutes after seven, the game commenced. The opponent had obviously decided to get a strong start, and during the first five minutes, I had faced eight shots already while we hadn't had any.

Then, our fourth line was given a chance against their fourth, and Reubens passed the puck to Woe, who scored into the upper corner of the goaltender's stick hand side. It was our first shot, and it silenced the audience for a while. I was happy I had given them the advice. We played with the same score on board through the first two periods. Midway into the third, it was the same pair again. This time Woe passed and Reubens scored into the low corner. Now I knew we had beaten them for sure.

It ended 2–0 for us, and our folks' Stanley Cup dream was alive. Again, I had faced one and half times more shots than Alabama goalie, Luke Thorpe. The Moonwatchers had a 3–2 lead in games now. In the press interview, the opponent's coach vowed that if they have to take it to the game 7, it would a different ballgame. I was already determined not to allow any goals. I didn't wanna be a hero, but I simply loved my city and wanted them to feel good.

The flight back went amazingly fast. I had a book about Native Americans' birth, adolescence, marriage, and funeral rituals; the different tribes' native words specially fascinated me. Some of them were so close to one another, some of them very unique. Overall, languages have a mysterious connection if you know how traditions, pronunciation, and seclusion affects them. I contemplated it would be fun to time travel to their era and try to communicate with them. I woke when they announced we were preparing the landing procedures and were exhorted to buckle up. It was clear, and while getting down, we could see a couple of cranes in one construction site. They made me nostalgic. But perhaps this summer I could work there for a while, just for a therapeutic purpose.

We arrived home by noon, thanks to the time difference. There were journalists and cameras waiting like we were champs already. I guess it was a slow news day, or did this puck-chasing hobby really turn them lunatics? It took us half an hour to get through. Finally at home, Gina had made oatmeal porridge for lunch, and it tasted celestial. What would I eat if oats didn't exist? Perhaps buckwheat. I decided, next time, we would try it with the Scandinavian method, made in the oven as a casserole.

After two days' rest, we were in action again. Most of the people came early to our last home game of the season. When we entered the arena for a pregame warm-up, the stands were three-quarters full already. Normally, it starts to fill up at the time of the national anthem. I saw a "Sherwood Will Bring Cup to Us" sign behind my goal. I also spotted Pro-Con's sign again and knew that my construction buddies were there for me too. I just would not have heart to let them down now. Igloomakers were in a good breeze, and the noise would easily beat a jumbo jet taking off. It was impossible to hear any announcements, but luckily, there were big screens to help out.

The opponent was overly aggressive and thus were given plenty of penalties. So we grabbed our every opportunity and scored twice in each period and beat them, 6–0. There was a huge party well after the game in the stands. It looked like people didn't want to depart. Now the games were even, 3–3, and we had only one decisive game left. What if I made one crucial mistake? This thought occurred to me the first time. The championship-defining game was to be three days later on Saturday in Alabama.

After all the media hoopla, we could finally go home half an hour later than normally. We had a day off again, and it felt good to sleep in. I woke up at ten thirty into the smell of oatmeal porridge. Gina served it with cinnamon and vanilla sauce and gave me a totally new taste experience. The rest of the day, I relaxed by reading and watching TV. We went for a walk and later invited the Braithwaites over. They were a happy retired couple who had lived a low-profile life with not plenty but enough to get by fine. I admired them and their life and wondered when was our chance to be a private couple. I also appreciated the fact that they didn't mention the words hockey or Igloomakers or Eskimos even once.

I realized somehow I was thinking hockey in my free time for the first time. Seemingly, the importance of the game had finally hit me. We headed back to Montgomery for game 7 the next afternoon. We arrived only at eight o'clock, and we were given a ten o'clock curfew. This meant serious business. At eleven in the morning, we had a strategic meeting that lasted for forty-five minutes. We were shown some film clips about the Moonwatchers' tactics and main scorers' tricks, which even I watched this time carefully. After this, there was a voluntary warm-up skate, which over half of the players participated. I didn't because I had never done it voluntarily before either. I waited for them in hotel to have a lunch together.

Next, we were taken to a ninety-minute city tour. I guess it was meant to take our minds out of hockey and an imminent final game. It was lovely; we were shown the state Capitol first, and only a block away, there was the First White House of Confederacy where President Jefferson Davis had lived with his family. Now it's a little controversial

JONATHAN RIIKONEN

history. We rode to see both upstream and downstream of Alabama River and also went to the outer county to get a glimpse of the rural side.

The rest of the day was free until 10:00 p.m. again. I went alone to the Alabama River and saw a couple of fishermen. The other one looked like a Chinese immigrant. Then I walked slowly to the White House and Capitol again. I stopped in a diner and a coffee house along the way. I came back at five thirty and stayed the rest of the night in hotel. I had requested my own room, and it was granted; thus, I had my own privacy. We had a dinner together at seven, but I didn't eat much since I had had two light bites already.

Even though a full moon was rising, I slept like a log until nine. I went to our own breakfast cabinet, where most guys were finishing already but still hanging there as accompaniment. My coach asked how I felt, and I convinced him I was as good as ever. Still in my subconscious mind, I pictured it was going to be a tough night. That day, we had a mandatory half-hour noncompetitive skate, and even I was ordered to take part. I semireluctantly did it, but knowing it was our last for three months made me accept it. It was not a problem to stand there but to put the goalie gear on and off. After this, we had a big late lunch, and most guys had a nap or just a rest in bed or in an armchair. The H-hour was at five, and we arrived to the rink an hour and half earlier. I could sense nervousness from some guys, but usually, it went away as soon as the battle began.

And there we were, in front of twenty thousand spectators and millions strong of TV audience, the nation's sports focus was almost exclusively on us. Whichever team won tonight would be a new Stanley Cup champion. An expansion team had never won the cup in their first season, not even reached a conference final. When I skated to my goal net, I got both cheers and whistles from the locals. I knew they wanted to win, but perhaps some of them had tacitly quit the hope already.

Our last fight started when the referee dropped the puck, and simultaneously, the noise commenced. I had to wait for three minutes until I faced the first shot, but ever since, the opponent dominated the game. Our guys had trouble getting the puck to the opponent's zone. The first period ended with shots, 19–6 for them. During the intermission, our coach exhorted to intensify the defense and give longer passes to the forwards.

However, whatever we did, the same pressing continued during the second period. We entered into the third still scoreless, 0–0, and both sides desperately tried to score. When the regulation was over, I had faced already forty-seven shots versus the opponent's sixteen. Ahead was looming a sudden-death overtime. We all ate some snack to keep us going and wiped sweat away from our faces and necks. Usually, I didn't sweat much, but now I felt some perspiration on me too. The coach told them to give shorter shifts whenever possible in order to maintain more speed.

The first overtime period was vivid; both teams moved a lot, but most shots were blocked, went by, or simply nullified by turnovers. The only stats for the periods were four shots from us and six from them and one penalty to each team. We had normal twenty-minute breaks. It felt good to come back since the ice surface was Zamboni-ed or resmoothed with a special machine with the brand name Zamboni. For the first few minutes, the puck slid easier and didn't get abrupt unpredictable bounces. We lasted another twenty minutes; now Moonwatchers had twelve shots against our five. We had played net one hundred minutes of hockey already, and both teams were getting tired. Also, I felt a little drowsy and took two cans of Coke to keep alert.

Soon began the third period overtime, and as we went through it, it meant we had played a double header of two full games. I faced a few really hard shots, but they were easy to stave off. Also, our guys had a couple of great chances, but it didn't go in. Obviously, they were determined to fight to the bitter end. Toward the end of the period, everyone was seemingly tired, only driven by unyielding nature and the trophy waiting in the hall. When the siren called, everyone was relieved to have a little rest. The game had lasted five hours already.

The twenty-minute break went amazingly fast, and we were back on ice. For the first five or so minutes, the game was faster again, but soon they started to tail away. I had faced a couple of shots from close distance, but since I knew where they were coming from, they were easy to stop. Then there was a volley-like slap shot that I picked with my glove and hit it to the center ice with my stick. The puck bounced over one enemy stick and landed straight to our Finn. He shot it right away "eyes closed," as he later described, and it landed into the net. That was it.

A huge "oooooh!" was heard from the crowd, and then our team started a wild dance. All our guys rushed to the ice, and scorer Kaapo Wirtanen was piled up with players. I just stayed there serenely thinking that, finally, our season had come to an end. Next, they rushed toward me and surrounded me like a guru. I felt embarrassed but happy for the guys who had dreamed about this moment. Soon our captain was presented the Stanley Cup, and everyone lifted it by turns, me also. I got the hugest cheer from the spectators. There were cameramen everywhere; there were gloves and sticks lying around. I could see the Montgomery players' heads down. I knew I had indirectly caused this pain for them. Obviously, everybody was taking this very seriously and reacted that way too. I was announced the MVP of the playoffs.

In the interview, I had to remind that I didn't score any goals, and it should be those guys rewarded. The media wanted to know how I felt and what would I do next.

"I will stay away from all sports grounds, gyms, arenas, and TV sports programs for the next three months," I answered.

What about my summer training program? I said I had never trained before either and was not planning it now either. Lastly, they inquired how I was going to celebrate, and I said that maybe have a plate of oatmeal porridge and apricot jam. Also, the tradition is that every player can have the cup for one full day. I said I'd give it to the children's hospital or something since it was a toy anyway. I guess this astounded media people a little.

In the hotel, I had many phone messages, calls, and texts waiting. I decided to turn it off and only gave Gina a quick call. I told her not to be too proud, only contented, it's all over for a while. She understood and told me she had bought me a gift. I said it was very thoughtful of her and I couldn't wait to see it. We flew to Santa Barbara next afternoon. When we entered the waiting hall, it was packed with people. Many flights had to be delayed since passengers couldn't get through. There were signs and banners welcoming us and giving compliments to me. Why not others also? Luckily, at least one praised Finn's game-winning goal.

The next morning news was full of excerpts of our games, my saves, and also a story on how they doubted when I was selected number 2 overall in the draft. The morning paper had a full front-page picture of me carrying the Stanley Cup. I also learned that the Stanley Cup parade was to be on Saturday four days later. Gina's gift for me was a headphone player and CDs of three new baroque music ensembles. I took them happily; it was my favorite music, and now I could listen to it everywhere. That afternoon I decided to go to see my mom's new pool. There had been too much distraction before. It was almost ready with plumbing and sewer, but the yard part and installing the slide were still in progress. I was happy that my mom talked most about the pool and not about our hockey achievement. She knew better already.

*   *   *

Later on in the afternoon, Willie Steele called and invited me to the contract signing that was going to happen live in front of the media next morning. With mixed feelings, I went there in the nick of time to avoid meeting my agent beforehand, and the flashlights were blinding even before it officially started. The CEO of Igloomakers, Mr. Stuyvesant, spoke first. He extolled my talent and thanked me for my contributions and repeated that it was only me who had brought the cup to Santa Barbara, and they were more than happy to make a long-time commitment with me.

Next orated Steele, who claimed this championship and now contract was because of his hard work. He disclosed I was to get one hundred million during the next five years or an average of twenty million per season. First, I would make sixteen, then eighteen, twenty, twenty-two, and finally, twenty-four million. That would be unprecedented in hockey history, but I deserved every penny, he claimed. We also knew that his cut would be a million a year, probably Steele's driving force. Then he invited me to say some words of gratitude.

I hated to be there. I scorned Steele's arrogance. So I rose and mentioned that this time a year ago, I hadn't played any NHL hockey, but now I had some. Then I disclosed I was first considering quitting, which raised a din in the room, but added that I decided to continue only for the sake of my city.

"To me, hockey has always been a hobby, just like chess or knitting or sculpting. And I think that's the way hockey should be: a hobby. So I'll agree to play for a full $100,000 a year," I declared and tore down the contract paper.

I almost got blinded from the camera flashlights.

"What!" shouted my agent, astounded.

I went on to explain that "A hundred thousand a year for a hobby is awfully a lot of money. I think street sweepers, nurses, or bus drivers do much more valuable work, and still, they have to work four years to earn this much. With the money the team can save, I think they should lower the ticket prices. But I'll take a couple of million for my foundation also, not as a salary, but as a direct contribution."

A red-faced Steele rose and shouted that I was a total idiot.

"I'll never forgive you for this. I took you to this level, and what I got in return was an ultimate insult. Not only me but all the other aspiring hockey players also. You traitor! I wouldn't care less if you'd be run over by a train!"

That said, he walked out while cameras were rolling. Mr. Stuyvesant picked up the microphone and said they were very pleased with my modesty and referred to me as a role model. He promised they would write a new contract accordingly very soon. I appreciated his words. Again, that night the news main topic was my contract. When would this end?

I didn't read the morning paper because I knew everything already. Gina went to bake with my mom to make some muffins for a charity sales table. I took my new headphone CD player and told them I would go for a meditation walk. I was now free and decided I wouldn't be in the headlines until the new season started. However, I was unfortunate enough to cause another sensation. But now I walked to the outskirts of town to the industrial area. The baroque sounds carried me like the time was flying. I didn't even realize I was doing real exercise.

I saw the old railroad that was once in a busy use, but now once or twice a week, an industrial train went there. Not even the rails were shiny from lots of use. I remembered when with youth pal, Bob, we walked side by side on the rails, competing who could walk longer without falling. Sometimes we were forced to jump out because a whistling train came. Now there was not that problem. This balancing made me nostalgic. I was lost in memories.

Somehow in my subconscious mind, I heard the familiar train whistle. First, I thought it was part of the music I was listening, then that I was imagining when I heard it longer. Was I returning to my long-lost early teenage years this vividly? After the third whistle, I turned around and saw a train engine only a few feet from me. I had gotten used to reacting quickly, so I tried to dive to the embankment. The last thing I remember was something hit me hard.

I was staring at white light, and for a fleeting moment, I thought it was in the end of tunnel, but actually, it was a hospital ceiling light. I felt a ghostlike pain in my left leg. Next, I saw a sobbing Gina next to me. I said faintly, "Hi."

She lifted her head from the handkerchief, and the first thing she said was "I shouldn't have given you the headphone player. It's all my fault!"

I reached for her hand and said all would be okay and that it was my silly idea to return to some youthful fun. Gina looked at me with an expression I had never seen in her before. It was almost an indescribable concoction of incredulity, despair, and cluelessness.

She lifted my blanket, and only then I could see I had lost my left leg.

"It was so badly maimed that they could not rejoin it to your body."

It was funny, I felt pain where my ankle and knee used to be even they weren't there. My first expression was "Wow, I don't need to play anymore. I don't need to be in the spotlight. I am free! This is probably the best thing that has happened to me since I met you."

I smiled at Gina, and she forced a smile back at me.

"You find something nice to say even in a terrible tragedy."

I said I'd get a prosthesis and would be able to walk again with crutches. Now I could do anything: go to the Himalayas and buy or set up a little green tea plantation and enjoy the fresh mountain valley air far from media hoopla.

I was hospitalized the third time within six months already. This time I was scheduled to spend ten days in intensive-care unit and then the rest of the recovery at a recuperating facility. The following day, our assistant coach, Sid Ek, paid me a visit. He was a class act; he didn't speak about the loss for the team but worried if I would be okay for the rest of my life. I convinced him I felt as good as ever, and he complimented my positivity.

Then Ek promised I would get my salary for the next four years as agreed. I didn't think it was necessary, but he insisted. He also had an idea that I could become their goalie coach, but I refused, stating that I couldn't convey my skills to anyone else, and besides, I claimed I didn't know anything about hockey. He understood and left me wishing well and deplored I couldn't attend the Stanley Cup parade. I saw a piece of it on TV.

The third day, I really started to comprehend what had happened. My life would change dramatically. While pondering this, I had another visitor. He was Kaapo Wirtanen, who was still in town because of the parade.

"How is our hockey pool king?" he greeted me teasingly.

I was elated to see him. He gave a gift to me, a book of ten dialects, synonyms, antonyms, and phrases in Finnish. It was one of the most awesome gifts I had ever received. He was contented I liked it. He was heading there for the summer season and invited me to stop by anytime, any year I happened to be around. I promised to take him up on that. I felt he was my only real hockey friend; I had been distant to anyone else.

My mom also came later and brought me a book about tea cultivating. She knew I had dreamed about it a long time. Her pool had been finished, and she had had her first slide into the water already. She was beaming with happiness. In spite of everything, I felt life was treating me well, and I had a fair share of everything. The next day I had my first day on crutches with the help of a nurse. First, I almost toppled a couple of times but soon learned how to balance. Later on, I was measured by a special prosthesis technician for my replacement leg. My ghost pain still continued, but it was subsiding already. I had a funny dream though: I was playing a hockey goalie, and I seemed to have three hands: one for stick, one for glove, and one bare hand for catching butterflies from the air. Yes, butterflies!

My artificial leg was fitted on the sixth day. The wound had healed as expected, and it was attached to the stump of my leg. I tried to walk and could take a couple of steps with the help of crutches. Again, I had to show up and perform four-legged walking that day for the media. It was the second time they were let in. In the *Santa Barbara News and Gossip,* I was portrayed as a brave and unyielding hard-luck fellow and a soldier of heroism that had an untimely and unfortunate end. I always shied away of being a hero. I didn't read more but instead studied every detail from the tea farmer's guide book.

I was released from rehab and had got used to my new self quite quickly. Besides, I was enjoying my freedom and being a private person again. The days went by on their own. We went for little walks every day, sometimes to have a lunch or snack in the city park. But it was hard to stay an unknown there because of my crutches and since Gina was also well-known in town by now. Many people stopped to give their condolences and well wishes. It wasn't too much fun, but then again, it wasn't a nuisance either.

*   *   *

In late July, I was declared healthy, considering the conditions, and I was cleared to travel by plane. Immediately, I started to plan our trip to Darjeeling, India, where there lived a small Sanskrit-speaking community. As I was fluent in the language, it would be easy to take care of things and find a place of our own. We packed a container full of clothes, basic necessities, and dearest things, mostly Gina's, had it shipped to a property agency's address there, and rented out our Californian home to a nice young couple and flew to Delhi on August 2.

After two days' recovery, we took a train toward Darjeeling. We had a first-class ticket, and I felt guilty, seeing how most people jammed into third-class cars. We were carried drinks and snacks by a turban-wearing waiter. The sceneries changed many times during our nine-hour trip. We could see the Himalayas' slopes from afar, and when closer, the area turned much lusher.

Some fifty-five miles before the destination, at New Jalpaiguri Junction, we had to change into a famous Toy Train, which is only a two-foot narrow-gauge rail line, declared a UNESCO World Heritage feature in 1999. What is more, it starts at 328 feet and finishes at 7,218 feet. Along the way, there are uncountable bridges and tunnels, steep curves, and some breathtaking sceneries. One can see tea plantations everywhere and some growers or farmhands pushing hand carts. Also, I spotted a few tractors in the scenery.

We exited the second last stop of the Toy Train line in a big village or little town of Jor Bungalow with about a thousand people. The air was warm but felt fresh and pure. I liked the atmosphere right away. There were some old British-style colonial houses, and we found the real estate place after asking instructions from the first villager. Mister Singh welcomed us and offered green Darjeeling tea and some sweet

JONATHAN RIIKONEN

cookie-like candies. He had two alternatives for us. We took a taxi to make a tour and also see a little around.

The first candidate was a twelve-acre plantation two miles away from Jor Bungalow. It had a three-room, two-floor rock house, and most of the tea plants were quite old and, so to speak, had seen their best days already. The asking price was equivalent to $65,000. The other one was just outside the town; it was two acres smaller, but three quarters of the plants were young and approaching their prime. The wooden house was built on sturdy stilts, and there were terrace decks on two sides. Gina fell in love with it immediately, and also its proximity to the town made it more attractive. The asking price was $89,000, but Mr. Singh said we could get it easily $5,000 cheaper.

I said that we would not haggle because they deserved a fair price, and he only nodded, and that was it. I signed the documents, and then we were happy owners of a tea farm. Also, the agent suggested we could hire the same two hands they had had before for only $1,200 a year. I promised to do it but already decided to pay them $2,500. When we met them and told them the news, they stared at us eyes wide, and then the other one came to hug me with tears in his eyes. We hired a cleaner to tidy up our new quarters and paid equivalent of $20 for a two-hour job. She curtsied as deep as if we were a royal couple.

Mr. Singh became our unofficial purveyor and advisor of whatever things we needed. He also spoke broken English, so Gina could follow the conversation. She had already learned how to say good morning (*suprabhaatam*), thank you (*anugrhitasmi*), or bye (*punardarsanaya*) in Sanskrit. Then came fall and a little cooler air, but the mountain actually kept our climate moderate because without it, all the northern currents could push frost and snow to the area. The whole Himalayan range was formed millions of years ago in a huge natural catastrophe when two tectonic plates from opposite directions collided and pushed the earth upward, forming the highest peak on the globe as a by-product. This explains why they have discovered loads of seashells at twenty thousand feet.

We learned all the tea cultivating procedures quickly. During the harvest, we hired housewives as helping hands and, of course, paid them double. When the word spread in the village, soon everyone wanted to work for us. I didn't aim for any profit, just to run it as a hobby and to make enough to cover the costs. I didn't do much, just walked around and chatted with my workers and village people and, of course, drank a lot of tea.

Young boys and also some girls played field hockey there, a local favorite sport. When they eventually heard about my past, they put me standing at the goal to stop their shots. It felt okay even with my leg prosthesis since I used one crutch as my support. I never let any goals no matter how hard they tried. It was fun because I knew that was everyone's hobby. Nobody planned to become a pro or a national level player.

I heard that Eskimos' first season didn't go as well as our first. They were third last in the league but had a good chance to select an able young player in the draft. A year earlier as champions, they could pick only as number 30. They had chosen an Italian-born Luigi Benetton who hadn't yet made the roster. This much I knew from news pieces from here and there.

Gina wanted to visit Santa Barbara, but I decided to stay here, and we planned she would return together with my mom. I saw her to the station and sent a big pack of fresh tea for her friends and our old neighbors. Ten days went quickly. I didn't do much, just hung around and read local history books I found from the store. Before Gina and Mom came, I hired the maid to clean and do grocery shopping and to cook a welcome meal.

They came by taxi from the station; it was a warm reunion. My mom looked much younger and healthier, and she liked our place right away. I took her for a tour with a golf cart I had acquired and told her the secrets of tea cultivating. One day we hired a driver to take us to the slopes of Himalayas, so high that we could overlook the whole Darjeeling area. Actually, some tea farms undulated on the slopes up to that level too. Once a week, we played field hockey with the kids in our front yard. My mom and Gina followed us from the terrace above.

Then it was time to leave. We all took train rides to New Delhi, this time an overnighter, and spent three days in the crowded capital. I didn't care for it too much, but the ladies spent hours shopping in the bazaar. After visiting Laxminarayan Temple, Lodi Gardens, Mehrauli Archaeological Park, and Nehru Memorial Museum, we decided we had had enough culture. We spent the last day just at the hotel pool and walked around a nearby upscale area.

*   *   *

The next four years were the happiest in my life. Of course, I missed my mom and we called once a month, but she was doing all right and had even found a special someone. I learned more about tea growing secrets and had an actively easy life. I had probably read half of the books in the library. We knew many villagers and even dined with a couple of families occasionally.

Then one day we were playing field hockey again. It's played with a cork ball covered with plastic, leather, or thread and a wooden stick with a curve in the end. The goalie stick resembles its hockey equivalent. There were ten or twelve kids playing for fun, usually three defenders and the rest attackers. I was always the only goaltender.

From our yard, we could have a good line of sight far along the straight plantation road. That day, I spotted a familiar figure appear in the end of the road. I just couldn't figure out who he was. He walked slowly toward us, and I stopped playing and just stared. Someone scored the first time, and they went wild for a minute, but then, all of the villagers gathered around and we all just observed. I called Gina's attention from the terrace too. When he was some fifty feet away, I realized it was my agent, Willie Steele. How on earth was he there and why?

He stopped about ten feet from me, smiled the first time, and said, "I guess it doesn't matter to you, but you were just selected to the Hockey Hall of Fame."

I shrugged and replied, "I didn't know that they had a field hockey Hall of Fame!"

Mr. Steele grinned and came to hug me.

"Oh my gosh," I heard Gina sigh.

I guess finally, all was forgiven.

CPSIA information can be obtained
at www.ICGtesting.com
Printed in the USA
BVHW070944240619
551797BV00007B/309/P